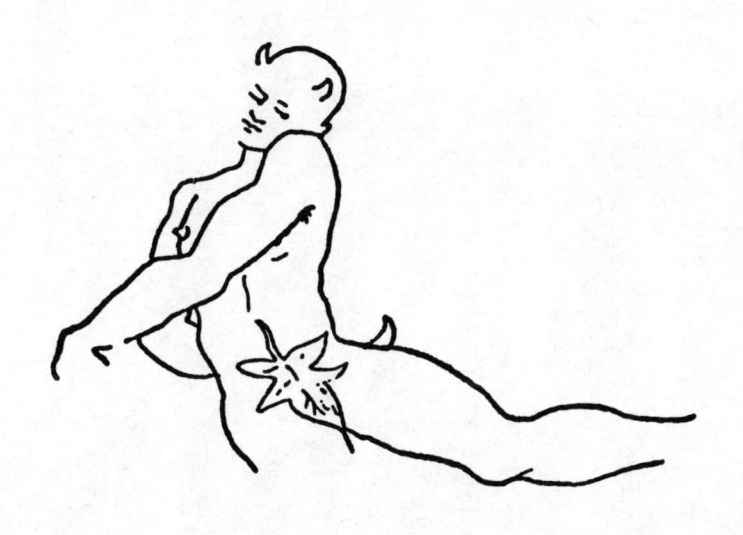

Inhabiting Shadows

BY THE SAME AUTHOR

Poetry

Bleecker Street
By the Fisheries
Nero
Selected Poems
Engaging Form
Nineties

Fiction

The Lipstick Boys
Blue Rock
Red Eclipse

Non-Fiction

Madness – The Price of Poetry

Jeremy Reed

Inhabiting Shadows

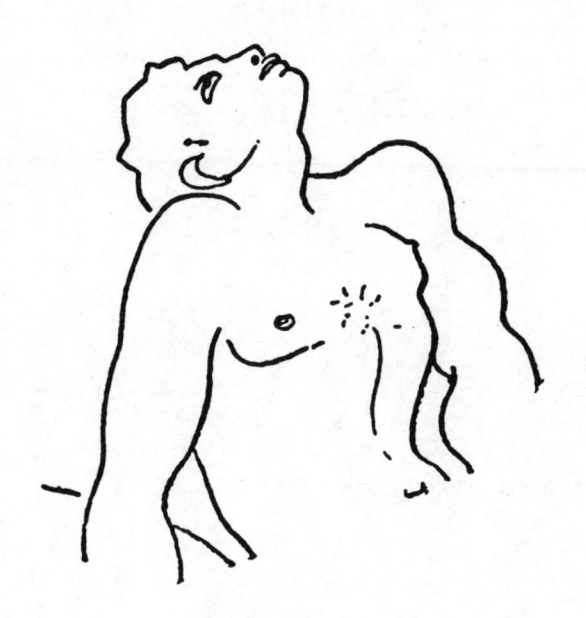

PETER OWEN
LONDON & CHESTER SPRINGS PA

PETER OWEN PUBLISHERS
73 Kenway Road, London SW5 0RE
Peter Owen books are distributed in the USA by
Dufour Editions Inc Chester Springs PA 19425 – 0449

First published in Great Britain 1990
© Jeremy Reed 1990

All Rights Reserved.
No part of this publication may be reproduced
in any form or by any means without the
written permission of the publishers.

British Library Cataloguing in Publication Data
Reed, Jeremy
  Inhabiting Shadows.
  I. Title
  823.914 [F]

  ISBN 0 – 7206 – 0787 – 6

Woodcut illustrations by Jean Cocteau

Printed in Great Britain by Billings of Worcester

For Alan Detweiler

I wish I could change my sex as I change my shirt.

André Breton

Part One

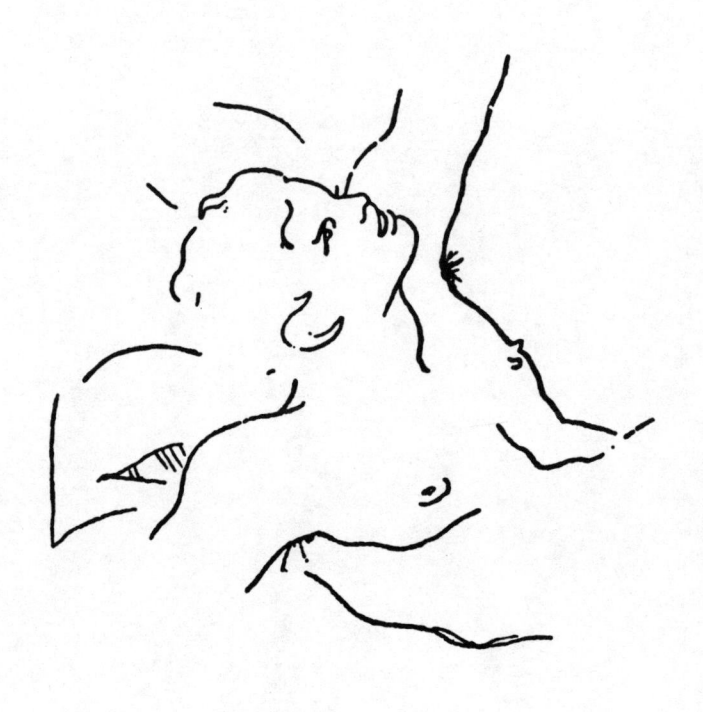

Chapter 1

That summer the heat was blond, leonine, and furnaced without respite. The dog-days were a blaze of embers; if you closed your eyes and listened, you could hear the sun's roar. The sun seemed to have shifted its location in space and drawn nearer to the earth, which followed its scarlet ellipse. It was red and black behind the eyes as though a second sun had assumed its perigee in inner space.

We were a circle who used these rocks, a conclave known to each other by a collective sympathy, an intuitive trust in a way of life that placed us outside the conventional social pattern.

When I stood looking out to sea, the horizon was ultramarine and cobalt, while the inshore channels were azure and turquoise, black where the shoals revealed their underwater fauna, the billowing sea-bushes of black and crimson weed. At low tide the reefs were exposed; they raised their serrated fins and spires as far out as the eye could travel. Occasionally a figure could be seen climbing from one gully to another, disappearing into a granite conclave, naked, oiled, sun-hatted against the white glare. It was a territory for men; someone had assiduously marked up MEN ONLY in white painted capitals on the inshore rock-faces, and it stood out, a defiant, block-faced proscription to warn intruders away.

Dione used to wait up in the gardens under the vined architrave of a sun-shelter, and from that height could monitor all those who dropped down to the shore under cover of tamarisks and the straggle of oaks that jutted seawards from their secure earth foundations. His *diamanté* drop-earring flashed in the sun; his matelot's blue and white striped T-shirt dropped diagonally from one bronzed shoulder, and the mould of his denims bottled the curve of his legs. He wore a red cummerbund, which dramatically accentuated his slimness. He missed nothing. He carried a whistle in his pocket which sounded eerily through the gulleys at night as a warning sign that danger was imminent. You'd hear it on still days when the tide receded so far that it was a luminous sheen in the sky, a mirror lifted to the blue sky-ceiling.

Dione was the eldest in our circle. His femininity was pronounced by the measured flicker of his blue-black eyelashes, stiffened by mascara to the brittleness of a paintbrush. His nervousness was evident in his eyes, that restive focus which wouldn't settle but looked all the time for invisible support, so that his gestures seemed to summon a posse of body-guards. He was the only member of our group who never swam. While we dived into the clear shallows he stood off at a distance, maintaining an angular pose for a concealed camera, his profile framed against a backdrop of rocks.

There were four of us who came here, our transistors alive with the immediacy of pop music or slow, nasally drawled blues, a saxophone blown to a cornucopia of blue roses, evoking in us the picture of a vocalist backstage making up with a trembling kohl-liner, tented in furs, a drug-need pronounced in the staring eyeballs. We all waited patiently for the transsexual narrative of 'Walk on the Wildside', Lou Reed's monotonal understatement of 'he was a she' hardly rising above the spoken word and creating for us the atmospherics of a New York screaming into the unremitting sky-blaze. White cubes banded with windows, a singer in shades and a floppy black beret slouched on a leather sofa, while up above a stockbroker teetered on a fire-escape, still half uncertain whether to pitch over into the canyons of metallic traffic. Jackie Curtis, Candy Darling, Sugarplum Fairy and Holly: we revered their life-styles, the agonized dilemma of the Factory transvestites, all compressed into the casual lyric narrative.

Dione was the first to speak of marrying a man. He had received proposals which he turned down because they lacked the material security of money. He spoke of Midas, a man who could turn stones and the ash left by a bonfire into gold. Such men existed in his philosophy as the autocratic tyrants who showed their fangs to all ivory-tusked contestants, but who essentially were feminine, passive, desperately seeking to find a companion in the void. He spoke of loneliness as a hole which widened with age, a gaping pit in which the feet became wedged, then the waist, and last of all the head. Death placed a stone on top of the skull, which was then crowned with a black flag.

I used to watch Dione's fingers ignite in a sparkle of faceted flashes. He could give a summarized biography of each of his admirers. The star sapphire came from a divorced Lloyd's underwriter who lived in a penthouse with an oval-shaped, black marble swimming-pool under cover of a conservatory. The emerald set with hexagonal diamond chips was an engagement ring from a septuagenarian admirer with stakes in oil. The various aquamarines and blue topazes came from an assortment of older men: a lawyer who left his practice and came out to these rocks punctually each afternoon, his pink button-down collar shirt divested of its tie; an architect; always professional men who had the means to buy Dione clothes and offer him a moneyed life-style in return for his body.

'One of us should get married out here on these rocks,' he would say. 'We could cool the champagne in the tidal swimming-pool, light fireworks, and the bride would wear a transparent black net skirt, with a pink rose in his hair.'

When the choral high camp of 'Walk on the Wildside' faded out to the accompaniment of the disc-jockey's brusque interpolation, we turned our attention to the beach. An incoming wave swung like a hammock before breaking into a lazy fish-net pattern of white racemes. On the other side of our rocks, divided by a stone jetty, were the unsuspecting beach colonies who worshipped the sun. Topless girls in microscopic black or white triangles luxuriated in the heat. One, a particular favourite of ours, would periodically sit up and check her cosmetics. Despite the torrid heat, she wore a livid red lipstick and brushed her blonde hair out in a firestreak of floating curls that hung suspended like an incoming wave in its brief, leisurely somersault. Her oiled tan was accentuated by a white beach-towel. The prowling wolves left her alone. She had an empathy with us that extended to a conniving wave of the hand, a recognition that we too could put on a face as we appeared and disappeared into the ivied recesses of the garden above the sea.

The four of us belonged to the same school, and had discovered this place at first separately, and then by one coming across the other, until our initial caution with each other had disappeared and we recognized a common concern in our still confused, half-formulated lives. The next summer would see an end to school and an eclipse of our freedom. On days when cloud shadows spotted the sand, making of the beach a Dalmatian's coat, I associated those dark intermissions with the future to come. Already we were figures on a speeded-up time-film, our lives overtaken in the act of our realizing that now, in the elusively unfixable moment of recognition, we had already passed on and would never be that again. And there was no way to oppose the wave, no force with which to break the white horses of incoming surf.

Dione, Nicholas, Paul and I – we were already speeding towards the great unknown with no brake applied to that acceleration. But the summer prolonged time. We could believe that we had entered a mythic age and that the sea-gods lived out on the rocks, blue-eyed, bronze-skinned, protean in their metamorphoses, but always immanent, hovering at the shoulder or appearing in a flash of heat lightning, a pressure in the incoming swell that seemed to mould itself to us while we were swimming, and entwine the blue feelers of the current around our naked bodies. Making love to water had the same exhilarative thrust and counterthrust as physical love – an ecstatic dynamic, the flickering of white sperm stars in the sea's blue ovum. Those seeds would animate the archetypal voyagers, Ulysses in his endless circumnavigation, crowding on sail in the doldrums, now taking the form of a dolphin in our bay, a grey mullet, a whirlpool, or the perfectly proportioned torso of an illusory Hellenic sunbather who disappeared on our approaching his sun-trap, leaving behind a tube of *Ambre Solaire*, a red beach-towel and a cryptically annotated copy of the *Greek Anthology*.

Once we were out in the gullies we were free. We seemed to have eluded the constraining anchorage of land and to exist in a series of mirror reflections. Echoes were amplified, the sound of a swimmer's overarm stroke broke the still surface with exaggerated labour, and more distantly voices reverberated from fishing-boats in the bay. A red, a white sail, erected sharks' fins on the skyline.

We had to restrain the impulse to float out on the tide. Its pull was magnetic, its flow irresistible, and sometimes the horizon appeared to be a proscenium on which the cast congregated, awaiting only our dramatical arrival, bodies sheathed in turquoise water, a smell of iodine and pine drifting on the sea breeze.

Dione introduced us to Max, who owned an exclusive fashion boutique in the sea-resort capital. His grey linen trousers and black shirt with its double button fastening offset the early silvering of his hair. His sun-glasses were raised into his frontal curls. Max wanted to take all four of us to the Aegean where, in Agena, he owned a white seaward-facing villa. He spoke of the silver olive groves, barbecues on the beach at night, the island excursions he would make available to us in his private yacht. But Dione wasn't impressed. He seemed to have sensed the fraud in the man and to flip it to the surface, so that it was discernible as a film on Max's skin, a tarnish that began to cloud his speech, diminish his stature and point to the visible rift in his being, the shadow, the night-wolf, the orbiting black satellite that lived in drift. Max was married and his secret life demanded the complicity of a double; his snakeskin wallet bulged with the money he thought necessary to attract prey. Rumours abounded of the twist in his nature, of his inherent feminine cruelty and the self-mutilating reprisals he brought against himself for his involuntary sexual propensities. He was consumed by hunger. He was like a man trying to put out a fire within himself but who succeeded only in fanning the blaze to eruptive lava.

We watched him go out to the rocks, inquisitive, scanning the bodies concealed on hidden ledges, until he too became a part of the light, the heat-wave that rolled in with the same pressurized momentum as the surf.

At the entrance to the beach, and wide of the granite steps hewn into the sea-wall, was the old coastguard's building which had fallen into disuse. Men came there at night, furtive, alone, seeking out the fraternity by cigarette-points, trust in the risk, stimulated by fear. It was then that one would hear

Dione's whistle pronounce a warning if he suspected the presence of the police, or sighted a white car, lights turned off and parked on the height above the bay. There were periodic arrests, and Max was one of the victims.

It had happened two years ago. His movements had been followed for weeks; a decoy had been used to create a scapegoat in an attempt to break up the colony. There were conflicting reports as to the latter's identity. A youth with hennaed red hair and high cheekbones who expressed evident curiosity rather than interest in a man who was kneeling at another's unzipped fly. The boy passed himself off as a seasonal hotel employee, someone still uncertain whether they would stay or migrate to a faster, more extravagant beach-set. They were always there, whether it was by the Aegean, the Adriatic, the Black Sea or the Mediterranean's languorous blue tidal pool.

Max visited the colony each night. He would leave his car parked by the old harbour works with its rusting buoys, ochre, metallic sea-pumpkins beached for respraying before being taken back to their stations by a pilot-boat. His temerity carried with it the recklessness of the sacrificial victim. If the warning had reached him of the danger inherent in approaching this youth, he had chosen to ignore it. Something about the latter's awkwardness, his fractional remove from what he saw and interpreted, his isolation no matter how he attempted to integrate, left him as an outsider, a mannequin whose attempted femininity was overpronounced. Max with his characteristic lack of caution took this for inexperience on the other's part. He must have planned his move for days.

Dione's whistle had already sounded on that suffocating August night. Something was in the air, a terror, a portent. It was the first time that the young man who called himself Gabriel had come here at night. I had seen him in lipstick and tight jeans slip out over the causeway to the nearest cluster of rocks. A lighthouse punctually asserted its white asterisk. A ship moved slowly across the skyline, its deck and windows lit up; bats undulated with abrupt elasticity from one oblique tangent to another.

Max must have followed him out to the rocks. I remember hearing someone's footsteps bite on the shingle before finding footholds on the spiny rocks. He must have got out to the first hollow which is concealed from the shore and dropped into the depression where Gabriel was waiting.

I pressed myself flat against the offside gable of the coastguard's house. Something was wrong. Dione must have cut across the beach and intersected with the promenade farther around the bay. There were four of them with torches waiting by the steps. I could see their dark uniforms, their peaked caps. Two of them went out to the rocks, while the other pair stood by the steps alert to the static crackle of transmitters.

I stood watching the beach break up into a snow of disconnected visuals. I shouldn't have been here in the blue-dark, my eyes sharply defined by a pencil, lips self-consciously parted as in a drawing by Cocteau.

Their voices were loud in the still night, I was paralysed into staying, as though I had to live the experience through and watch a man broken by his natural instincts. And if I ran, I'd be apprehended, for the only way out led up a tortuous path to the car-park where a police van was stationed. I could hear Max's uncoordinated step dragging behind Gabriel's as a consequence of his being handcuffed. One of the policemen was talking into his transmitter, his voice amplified in the echo-chamber provided by the rocks. Max came ashore, his head lowered, his bitter silence accentuated by his inner torsion. He must have been searching for an escape inside, twisting himself round for a direction, a way clear to a space where his captives couldn't follow. The two parties had separated into outer and inner space. They took him up the hill, a man who must have been thinking back to his last minutes of freedom, convincing himself that none of this had really happened, and that if he only stopped thinking for a moment the screen would clear and he would find himself standing alone, staring out to sea, the blue night touching his skin with the coolness of watered silk.

For the first time I realized the risk in our life-style, became aware of Dione's nonchalance and our emulation of his femininity. We had come to challenge existing values with narcissistic temerity, and we too could be broken in the way that Max had been shadowed and pulled out of the night on a chain.

My heart was taking big leaps as though it were propelling a mountaineer on a sheer summit-face. I was conscious that I had only myself in which to hide. I wanted to run but stayed. The lighthouse kept twitching, placing its punctual star inshore, a sort of mad eye timed by a spasmodic nerve. I must have stood there a long time, fearing anything and everything, before the sound of engines above me throbbed into life and a police klaxon started mewling as they headed back from the coast.

Max, who had been fined and cautioned, remained undeterred. Within a month he was back, and now two years later the scar was there as a shadow-pain he tried to conceal, only it stood out in the hesitant inflexion of his voice, the way he perfunctorily broke off a conversation. It was a contained paranoia that had him look over his shoulder. His hair had greyed, the dark shot through with silver, and he spoke of going to live in Greece permanently. We knew almost everyone by sight who visited the cauldron of rocks. Our strategic vantage-point in the gardens, looking down from a height, allowed us to monitor each arrival and departure. The sun was top-heavy, scarlet, brutally incandescent, so that one almost expected the pebbles on the beach to explode. Men were turning brown and then black in the marine hecatomb.

Dione kept out of the sun and wore a cream-based

foundation to protect his skin. Sometimes we looked like exhibits from a Venetian mask-maker's workroom, perfections of tweezers and brush, papier-mâché cut-outs painted white and black and red. There were so many variations of creating a face – it could be a Miro, a Man Ray, a Picasso, the hemispheres could complement each other or remain divided by the perceptible seam which marks the androgyne.

We were all waiting for something to happen, for the future to surprise us with the rush of a mercurial thunder-shower. Nicholas cared least about anything. He had his father's business as a lazy prospect, a sinecure which would allow him to travel. His father was in real estate; he bought up cubist high-rises and speculated on them until they turned into vertical gold bars. Nicholas was black haired and diminutive. He was so petite he gave the impression of having been formed for a compact world, one in which things were done on the perfectionist's scale of the miniature. Nicholas's world was the microcosm of a dollhouse. His gestures, like his looks, were concise. His life was measured by exact proportion. The tincture of Joy he wore was quantitatively matched by his ambience, three small droplets that defined the space within which he moved. He dressed unostentatiously but with the fastidiousness of a girl. He used to say, 'Even if my father knew, he would never disinherit me. I'm all he's got.' This was the reasoning to which he returned in times of threat when his usually unruffled nature felt exposed to public criticism. Our movements had not escaped notice; we were in danger of becoming known for our habits, our peculiar fascination with a place, which could only mean bad. 'You think I'm some sort of gay-glade/Then why don't you swallow a razor-blade?' Nicholas would sing mischievously, unable to recapture Lou Reed's vicious delivery.

We knew all his songs by heart. Somehow he gave voice to the whole issue of gender – 'Jack's in his corset/Jane is in her vest'. This peroxided leather cat pointed his black, varnished finger at the world from the core of a reverberating wall of sound. We imitated his upturned leather collar, his studded wrist-bands, but it was the sound we loved – the insurgent defiance, the amphetamine rush that threatened to break the sound-barrier. Uncle Lou's cool black shades and speed-freak monotone were a way of life. So too was the pink lipstick line holding together above a pancake bristled with blue stubble. We coveted the bootleg cassettes made of his live concerts, the improvisation that performance invited, the undoctored whiplash of guitars, Lou's obscene interpolations by way of angry rapport with the audience.

Paul was the one to whom none of us could get close, and yet virtues of loyalty and reliability made him the centre-pin of our small circle. He lived out on the north coast in a granite farmhouse with parents who came from a centuries' old farming tradition. Their insularity, pincer-locked parsimony and scheming intentions to marry Paul off to the daughter of a neighbouring farmer, in the interests of uniting the land, were pressures that lived forcibly within him. He had another two years' grace before the putative marriage became a reality; years in which he was inwardly desperate to find an escape, a way of life that would sever him from his origins.

Paul was big-boned, betraying his Breton origins, the beamed girth of his father, but his lips and eyes were feminine, as though part of him dissociated from his male physiognomy as an indication that year by year this split would grow more apparent – the masculine would be overtaken by the feminine, the body pivot on a finer axis, the features assume the confidence of one who had discovered his identity. It was his parents' naïvety that allowed him to join us at the colony. They assumed he was studying for his examinations in the library, and as they visited the town capital only once a year on Christmas Eve, they could not check on his extramural studies. His father employed minimal labour in order to exact higher profits. He was out in the fields at the first red streak of dawn and returned only when the frenetic zigzag of bats had replaced the frenzied dusk feeding of swallows.

Paul's nightly returns went unquestioned even if they were viewed with disfavour. I had the feeling that he nursed a slow-burning desperation, a fuse that smouldered on a two-year trail to the dynamited inner centre. He was outwardly placid; his demeanour was one of quiet equanimity. I could see he loved Dione in a way that would always remain unrequited. He was mesmerized by the latter's overstatement of the feminine, the values which were so alien to his own upbringing, the pinched girl's pink cashmere sweaters, the sexually provocative angled hand on one hip, the painted eyebrow that resembled a crescent moon standing on its arched head. The rejection he felt was the worse for being self-inflicted, for Dione in his narcissistic indwelling assumed that everyone desired him as a matter of course – he was the untouchable, the unattainable actress bustling in her silks towards a dressing room lined with mirrors and the hectic scarlet of tall-stemmed roses. The universally loved always reverted to the solitary – the face angled for self-admiration, the fluffy blue smoke-ring dispersing across the reflected features.

'Hey man/Take a walk on the wild side,' Dione would pout, and everything that should have been antipathetic to Paul and contradictory to his stolid upbringing was erased in a flooding of his green eyes, an internalization of the characteristics he so revered.

Dione wanted pleasure without commitment. His coquettish, hard-to-get womanhood was designed to attract the courtship of money and gifts without the concomitant sex expected on his part. He demanded things for being Dione. Rectangular bottles of Chanel No. 5, luxurious silk scarves, initialled cigarette-cases, he presided ever his loot like a boy Pharaoh in his funerary chamber surrounded by wig-boxes, amphorae, lapis lazuli scarabs, all the hoard that a barque could float in its navigation of the river of the death.

Someone paid for Dione to have a small town flat. His parents lived abroad in Malaysia, and he took advantage of the situation to adopt a life-style and precocity extraordinary for someone still at school. He was to be found in the Blue Mink at an early hour of the morning, his body subtilized by slow medleys, his gestures demanding an unequivocal devotion on the part of the waiters. He luxuriated in attention. He was like a houri, an odalisque, a Ganymedean catamite. The blue, mentholated smoke-rings he shaped from his carmine lips were gestures of boredom. He was surfeited with attention; he was one of those who ran to lose not win, simply as an expression of freedom. The holiday offers, perfumes, jewellery, had all grown to a sameness that he greeted with indifference. And together with this youthful adulation went the corresponding realization of premature age. It was as though Dione had consumed a lifetime in his eighteen years. He had burnt out the prospect of a future by his concentration on the present. Fearing age, he had anticipated and consumed it in a flash. By the time he reached thirty he would be sixty. I could see this in a way that Paul and Nicholas couldn't. They were blinded by the immediate, they didn't dare envisage an end to youth – the thistle developing a grey shako and taking off with the first puff of breeze.

It might have been this summer or the last that Dione had graduated to drugs. He needed kicks; implosive flashes to light up his sensory craving for experience.

> And when you cut that dude with the stiletto
> It was far better than sex.
> It seemed the final thing to do.

Again he took his lead from Lou Reed – he was looking for sensation to blow him out of the monotony of the present. Almost nothing touched him; his cool detachment was countered by a corresponding paranoia. He developed narratives of having been followed. His plots never rang true and always ended with the fabrication of his having had recourse to sex in order to disarm his pursuer. 'He told me that if I didn't blow his dingdong, he'd have me arrested for soliciting. And all the time I worked at him he was feeling for the sachet that lived in the back pocket of my jeans.'

He'd stand back from his words, convincing himself of what he'd said, as though he was hearing it from a stranger. There was a gulf between him and his language; nothing he said carried conviction – it seemed to emanate from a source that lived as a ghost between intention and meaning. Listening to Dione was like visualizing a series of mini-films in which he played the lead role.

That afternoon from the shade of our sea-garden shelter we watched the sun come closer. The air struck our faces like heat blown off a furnace-back. The summer was unreal; we stood in the blond heat-wave, half expecting to print our youth on the light. A tableau inscribed on the future.

We lived in expectation of the dusk, a blueing of the gold that brought strangers into our purlieu. As the light deepened, they became visible by the firefly glow of a cigarette, the strategic occupying of a position which was in itself a sexual come-on. Men came here and left without so much as a name or a telephone number given by way of exchange for physical pleasure. The more lonely left a cryptic code of contact scribbled on a wall or bench-back. We waited in the hope of meeting the elusive stranger who would alter our lives. The hero stepped out of a field of goldenrod, his lips tasting of pollen, his red, heart-shaped mouth causing women to look round in envy at the uncompromising pronouncement of his make-up. This man was always about to arrive – our lives were spent waiting for the big change – the window opening out suddenly to sun dazzle.

Chapter 2

The room was copper-coloured by the late sun. Jamie stood attitudinizing, back flat to the white wall on which a black rectangle had been painted. He had adopted the stance of the wooden artist's model, with its featureless de Chirico head, that stood vigil on the round, glass-topped table.

Dione lay on the floor in Turkish trousers staring up at the gold and silver inflatable mobiles that hung on short leads from the ceiling. They were shaped like missiles, and one day, in a state of exalted drunkenness, Jamie had given shape to his dream by unleashing a great number of metallic balloons from his balcony. They equivocated in the breeze before drifting out over the beach, a gold and silver one kiting across the bay, sun and moon in dramatic, eye-teasing orbit, finally lost in the expansiveness of the azure.

Jamie was a cosmetician or mask-maker, as he liked to call it. He lived for the big break – the improbable offer of work with a film or theatre company. He was kept by someone known to us as the Hornbill, a tall, sallow, jaundiced man with a scimitar-shaped nose, which seen in profile detracted from any other feature. The Hornbill specialized in stocks and shares, his myopia demanding the use of an eyeglass. Even on the coldest day in January, he was to be seen in shirt-sleeves, his thin body seemingly immune to the cutting wind. He and Jamie lived in separate apartments, his obsessive microphobia and round-the-clock international calls abnegating the possibility of a harmonious relationship. Jamie not only enjoyed a generous allowance but entertained great respect for his older partner, manifesting the extended tolerance one might show to an eccentric but kind father. Seen together they were an incongruous couple: the one effeminate, proud of the two rose tattoos on his bottom, a flower on each cheek, and the other prototypically masculine, outwardly straight, above suspicion in his conformance to the social protocol.

When Jamie didn't have models on which to practise his art, he drew the exhaustive variations of a face on blocks of paper. There were square faces, oval ones, angularly emaciated faces, triangular, vertical, hexagonal eyes, mouths in symmetrical opposition to facial planes, lips brushed into two tones, the upper gold, the lower black. Jamie was searching for a new face, one that could be painted on and later disposed of, and came up with the idea of using a tissue-thin, surgical-skin mask. This accessory, which in turn became an identity, was to be contoured to the subject's features. It would live on the skin, moulded by body heat, and be detachable by a small tuck under the chin. In this way the fantastical could be adopted and discarded. The cosmetic kit would allow for every conceivable design – harlequin extravaganzas, re-creation of Egyptian deities, the black and white matt coverage of a geisha, Martian speculations, faces depicting star maps, male and female accented in their respective counterbalancing roles in the one expression.

Jamie was obsessed with make-up. He dreamt of remodelling the face, drew androids with a single red eye on white balloons, dotted orange balloons with leopard-spot markings, colouring the slit eyes, one green, one purple. He studied the theory of niosomes – microscopic spheres that matched the skin's cellular structure and rebuilt tissue damage. He advocated cosmetic surgery for his older friends and spoke enthusiastically of collagen implantation which could restructure the natural ageing process, erasing eye depressions, corrugations, and restructuring the skin according to the expectations of youth. He would have agreed with Paul Valéry's remark to Coco Chanel: 'A woman who doesn't wear perfume has no future.' His bedroom was full of mannequins. Black arrows drawn on faces indicated the zones marked out for rejuvenation, muscle and fascia could be lifted, minimizing the distortion of the hairline. He spoke of rhinoplasty to lift the tip of the nose and implant corrections to restore the prominence of the cheekbones. He studied Picasso, Miro, Klee, Bacon, *haute couture* magazines, searching always for the impossible variant that corresponded to his vision. There were always girls in his flat, Rubella and Dolores, Francesca and Nicole, all of whom lived according to the dictates of fashion and intuited a corresponding femininity in Jamie's friends. They believed in unity, the interchange of gender that allowed for fluidity between the sexes, the braiding of masculine and feminine into one current – a white Ophelia on the black river, a midnight-blue shadow showing beneath her smudged foundation, one eyebrow pencilled into a crescent moon, the other unshaped, defiantly, broadly hirsute. Jamie gave parties to which Dione was invited. They were called Apocalyptic Mirrors, each guest being handed a mask on entry with which at some time in the course of the night they must confront themselves in the oval mirror placed in an ante-room. It was an initiation, an act of sober introspection that each underwent in privacy before returning to the loud music. No one spoke of this mystery – it was treated with awesome gravity – but everyone at some stage entered the privacy of that dimly lit room and locked the door for the revelation that came of being alone with a double. The ritual was the measure of Jamie's seriousness. It must have been the depth side of his nature that appealed to his older partner, not that the latter would have nursed any sympathies for so esoteric a practice.

The restrictions imposed on my own life by arbitrating parents made it impossible for me to attend Jamie's parties with regularity. On the few occasions I went there, I was aware of a suffocating ostentation of dress and mannerism. If the Hornbill made a brief appearance, it was to pursue so naturally distracted an orbit that he was considered to be the epitome of camp hilarity. His appearance fascinated. His wrongly put together clothes, his maladroit gestures in contradistinction to his impeccable manners, his quizzical air of self-absorption in public, his vaguely clipped, old-fashioned language, all of these characteristics were governed by an amiable eccentricity.

At the time I was set on writing outrageous lyrics for a still embryonic pop band. Dissonance, abrasiveness, a pyrotechnical Dada married to a romantic realism – I wanted my songs to have the impact of a stone thrown at a black glass. I imagined them sung by fighter pilots moving into the attack, or by a leather-clad girl stood on the Acropolis, while a helicopter unleashed a storm of roses through the cloud-frescoed azure.

Eventually Rubella performed two of my songs at a private audition at Jamie's. Dressed in gold stilettos and a black rubber mini-skirt, she performed Flip to a sleazy guitar.

> You flip her over man, she gives it back,
> flick up her skirt and her panties are black,
> when she's a he they're in leopard-skin,

> a lipsticked transvestite looking for fun,
> and the Egyptian gods stare from the sun.
> In red and black or gold and green
> one fits over and one between,
> Jane's an obsession and Zany's a queen,
> on Devil's Island they score peyote,
> explode their vision in the sapphire sea,
> their flip over is ecstasy,
> you flip her over man, she gives it back,
> flick up her skirt and her panties are black,
> you better read Louis Aragon
> before the sun blows up in megatons.

The song was wildly applauded, but more for Rubella's dance movements – her body accented by the constraint of a second skin, her delivery issued through overblown scarlet lips. For the encore she sang my 'Blood Roses', this time dressed in a black G-string with a red silk tie falling between her breasts. An off-beat cabaret piano twinkled to a lurching accompaniment.

> Since you went over
>   to another lover
> I lie on an ostrich-plumed bed,
>   Caligula, Nero,
> Oscar Wilde as a hero
>   of liberative sex
> is how we advance.
> But I'm here with my tableau
> of lost loves, my trousseau,
>   and I float in a vortex
> where drowned sailors dance.
> And I'd shoot myself in the head.
>   Jean Genet, Garcia Lorca,
> I offer you blood roses,

> Arthur Rimbaud, Paul Verlaine,
> I feel more than certain
> your lives knew a moment
>   outside such long torment,
> when the fire in your wineglass
>   was the red of the sunset;
> but since you went over
>   to another lover
> my heart's on a blade of regret.
>   I visit your gravestones
> in the rain and I'm alone,
> and I'd shoot myself in the head.
>   But I'm waiting for your dead hands
>   to hold mine in the sunshine,
>   waiting for a bracelet
> inscribed by Caligula,
>   Nero, Garcia Lorca,
> and for the red rose to open
>   in my own glass of wine.

Smoking a black Sobranie cigarette, and flicking the ash into the lining of a top hat stood on its head, Rubella luxuriated in the lyrics, in the roll-call of the dead, poets marked by their aberrant sexuality, an emperor whose extravagant perversity stopped at nothing – not even the apotheosization of his pets.

The enthusiasm expressed by Jamie's neophytes demanded that we take it seriously. Rubella wanted to call the band after Henry Miller's 'Max and the White Phagocytes', but eventually we settled on the Necrophiliacs, a name that was consonant with the death culture explored by our music. We envisaged ourselves as high priests of a black cult – we would raise the dead on stage in necromantic rituals, our performances pushing risk beyond every safety margin. Our impact would be lethal, insidious, dynamic, provocative. A circle of mannequins would guard us on stage. Gold heads on black bodies, they would represent a new species animated by our music, figures whom we had attracted from the still unrealized blueprints of future anatomies.

Rubella and I used to visit clubs at the weekend, but nothing met with our approval. The conformist hegemony were without outrage or individuality – their revolution was a compromise, their performers eased nonchalantly up to the safety net and patted it out of caution. We longed to get up under the spotlights and inject stimulus into the hidebound carcass of a dead elephant. Our songs had the dynamic knife-edge of demanding absolute attention or offended dismissal. Complacency, that soporific, cat-yawning malaise, was the indolent creature we were out to stick.

Most of the songs we listened to were elliptical in all the wrong ways, the connective leap being replaced by monotonous repetition. The quandary of a moody, blue-denimed boy growing progressively lonely on unrequited love, or the dilemma of a girl finding herself too shy to speak to the stranger fogged out by smoke-clouds across the bar, recurred with unctuous regularity, always A and B, black and white, the song staged not around the discord of irreconcilables, but rather the preconceived notion of happiness experienced by both partners in their conventional predicament.

We longed to transpose entertainment into an art form, to replace acoustic with epileptic guitar riffs, quotidian sentiment with surreal inventiveness. Fired by the novels of J.G. Ballard, the apocalyptic nightmare of Lautréamont's Maldoror, the delirious colour of Rimbaud's hallucinations, I projected towards a flaming black shore guarded by bird-shaped lighthouses, an island on which wild horses ran through the pink sea-mist, and the inhabitants lived on the blinding intoxicant of vision. In time it would grow into a novel. I thought of a vision as a sunflower seed; one swallowed it and the flower opened in one's mind and went on expanding until it became the great yellow fireball of the sun.

Rubella had already acquired the same reputation for shock as Dione. Her cut-out clothes, fish-net skirts, black and pillar-box red lipsticks turned every head in barracking opprobrium or shocked sexual curiosity. But she was untouchable to the outsider: her sympathies lay with the male who emulated her extravagance; she gravitated undeviatingly towards whatever face of the opposite sex mirrored her own. I can see her still, walking towards midnight in a skirt made of red tassels, her black seams taking the eye all the way up, her arms interpreting the song she sung in a rainy street, possessed by its rhythm, hands clapping like maracas.

Dione grew to be jealous of our act, which no matter how formative and restricted by funds, nevertheless threatened to upstage his exhibitionism. He became more financially demanding of his ageing circle of admirers. He boasted of never wearing a shirt twice – his button-downs came in every fabric and colour and he wore them with the sad expression of one who knew that only he was conscious of the caught, triple-buttoned cuff, the square rather than round mother-of-pearl buttons decorating a green linen front, the concealed motif on a pocket that represented the epitome of élitist fashion.

And while we were all searching for an extensible future, one which would telescope our inner lives into an outer reality, he contracted on his youth, hedged it off from possibilities of expansion, and blew on himself like a brilliant ember. He would have liked to look at himself the way one admires a precious stone. Dione was a diamond without light; he lacked the inner radiance to have himself shine, relying on others to do so for him.

We could none of us imagine him other than as he was. He had narrowed the possibilities of his life to a moneyed catch – a man who would keep him as a woman, only more luxuriously, for the instability in male relationships between old and young demanded a total uncompromising sacrifice on the part of the purchaser. Dione took a delight in that knife-edge tension. His power lay in the desirability of his youth, a prerogative he was determined to exploit with vicious recriminations against the old. If he lost his looks he would put his fist through the mirror rather than acknowledge it. We could gain no perspective on his future. Sometimes we would imagine him as an old man, grey haired, spindly, but with the same unageing, heart-shaped face that pleaded to correspond in years to his body, rather than remain an elegy for the dawn of poetry.

'Everything bores me,' Dione would repeat over and over, playing a fingernail into the light in order to look for flaws in the varnish. 'The music at the Three Diamonds lacks kicks, and that insurance queen, the one who comes here in the afternoons, wouldn't agree to a standing order each month. Imagine, I blew him like velvet for champagne and a taxi.' He made an expression of disdain by drawing in his lips and sticking out his nose.

Nicholas expressed a silent aversion; he harboured a dislike for Dione that lived just beneath the surface of his unfailing correctness. Nicholas would proportion his future to its expectations, in ten years time as a prosperous partner in the family business he would doubtless find himself living with a man, someone similarly fastidious, romantic enough to read Proust in a violet armchair by candlelight. He would come back here and remember youth and the siccative wind of a torrid summer, the imaginings under the shade of a mulberry tree, the starfish found in the blue gully, first promises, expectations, the timidity of backing off from love under the noonday glare, no matter the bronzed chest, the gazelle's eyes, a gold heart-shaped locket snapping at the mouth.

And Paul, with his deeper earth-roots that spread underground like a tree, and which were dependable like a centuries' old oak glade, his life would be the hardest, for he had the most obstacles to surmount. His life would be a slow coming to terms with his sexuality. If I imagined Paul returning here in later life, it would be clandestinely, leaving a wife asleep in a country bedroom, his good looks emerging from the shadows into the lights placed strategically beneath hydrangea bushes in our gardens. His form of sex would be dangerous and fast, his uptake immediate with the first stranger he encountered who manifested a similar need. The man would never even know his name; the casual anonymity of the encounter would engender its own excitement, and then he would be gone, a concentrated face behind a windscreen following the yellow wash of his headlights over granite farm walls, before he mounted the stairs he had come to know by heart, slackening his weight for the creaks in the boards, and finally lying down as if in a shroud beside his dormant wife. He would lie there a long time thinking into the dark, feeling the appeased glow in his stomach, recalling the years when he was free to contemplate a sun-struck future. There was Dione, Nicholas, myself, and. . . .

We were inseparable, more out of fear than love. Once we realized we were a minority, alienated by reason of our sexual orientation and life-styles, a bond grew up between us that only served further to accent our defiant vulnerability. We lived on the edge of ourselves and the sea. The dazzle of the incoming wave warned us of how close we had come to exchanging elements. The surf arrived as a beat of the universal rhythm – it extinguished itself at our frontier, almost emphasizing our counterflow, our cutting thrust against life. Shards of glass-green bottles, rusty cans, the amethyst carapace of a cleaned-out crab, an orange lobster-float, the debris of the void was jettisoned at our feet in a boiling, phosphorescent crest.

'I'd rather have an operation than be one of them,' Dione had sneered as a reference point to the world. He spoke of the ultimate transformation, the mutation of gender which would free him from the sex his parents had imposed on him. Electrolysis, silicone treatment, voice training – it was a way of being reborn, a revocation of inherited gender. Genetic blueprints, character types, Dione revolted against the ordinary. I remember the still afternoon we followed the ebb down, the gullies draining in forests of crimson and russet kelp, the reefs disclosed like totems in a Max Ernst, a green sun pursuing us, and Dione had broken free and stood on a pinnacle.

We watched him slip his black Turkish trousers to his ankles and stand there in white see-through briefs from which he disengaged to reveal the body paint he had used on his genitals. His cock was silver and his buttocks were one side silver, the other gold. He was like a failed Nijinsky, an exhibitionist who would undergo mutilation rather than conform. What Jamie imagined for the face, Dione had transferred to the erogenous zones. This was his narcissistic apotheosis, the cosmetic boy-god burning in the agonizing crucible of youth, conscious that his outrage would be repeated by us – it would travel like an airborne seed from tongue to tongue.

That was the afternoon we found the slatted boards of a dinghy which must have broken up on the rocks. Rough boards painted white which still seemed impregnated with the storm's smashing momentum. Paul decided to take the slatted timber back home. He would carve a miniature ship from these remnants of planking. It would be his own practical way of celebrating the dead.

Men had gone down even farther than us to an old lighthouse accessible only at the year's lowest tide. Gulls spun round its shaling cone, and low-water fishermen picked spider-crabs out of the weed tussocks. Dione said that couples had sex out there in the lighthouse just for the danger; the tide crept back with the cunning of a swimming fox, and then there was no return. You'd have to swim back across the dividing channels against a current lethal as a boa-constrictor.

We were tense, anxious with each passing day that the summer was nearing an end despite the relentless gold heat. There was a silence in the air as though the light in its falling had created a soundless vacuum. The sky was like a wheatfield; a lacquered red-gold glaze. But we kept waiting for the crash, the equinoctial thunder hoofs that would churn the sea to a black impasto. Rain would blotch the mulberry berries and strafe the white and red beds of petunias. We would be reduced to huddling in the garden shelter, smoking, projecting the architectonics of possible futures, thrown back on the old contention of how to make our fantasies live as realities.

'There's nothing I wouldn't stop at for highs,' said Dione. 'The rest of you don't know how to live.' He was bitter, contemptuous, anxious to shock by his disregard for individual rights. We drifted back to the shore, leaving him out there on his saddle of rock, his black, pencilled eyebrows arched for the inquisitive stranger. If the man lacked money, he would be consigned to Dione's morosely indignant silence; a mood that lived on the knife-flare of anger, the scream of the disappointed woman forced to live in the wrong body.

Chapter 3

Our town was a small one – the sea lived in its sky – a blue flag folded in the arms of another flag. After the day's heat we anticipated twilight – the expectation of shadows – the gunnels of small fishing-boats lit up under the arm of the South Pier, the lights coming on in town, red and blue and green.

It was a time of waiting, an hour to run a comb repeatedly through one's hair and to count up the fallen skirts of a rose which have scalloped a desk-top. It's as though the house is surrounded by black horses, each of which presses its head against the blueing glass. A time to make last-minute revisions to the poem written, and to sit imagining the great shapes that will evolve from the night. A yellow moon will appear like a porthole in the sky and naked swimmers slip into the warm sea under the stars.

In those late summer days we gave up our habit of going to

the gardens at night and slipped into a club called the Pink Lagoon. Rubella had a job there as a waitress, a gambit towards finding a spot as a singer on that small oval dance-floor with its alternating red and white spotlights picking out a couple of white-shirted boys dancing together through the intermediary of a girl spicy with Chanel pour Monsieur. The club was situated at the end of a cobbled alley leading off from the South Pier complex. When fog blew in off the night waters, hanging its chiffon scarves in the alley, we imagined ourselves as sailors in Genet's *Querelle de Brest*. We were sea creatures, shirts flaming in the fins of mist, our language secret as the blue leagues of ocean; we could roll a word like a pearl over an intimate tongue, and see it swallowed without anyone apprehending the gesture.

By the time Rubella had persuaded the club to give her a fifteen-minute soloist's spot, I had written a new set of lyrics, morbid, perverse, touching on a stray nerve that might jump like blue touch-paper into society's ossified crotch.

Rubella had waited for this chance to excel. She had lived through so many imaginary cynosures, the camera finding her out in a choreographed profile, a lip-hinged, menacing full-frontal, eyes closed, the mouth open like a rose cupping the microphone. Her life would be concentrated into the agonizing interpretation of lyrics that bypassed the small crowd. She would perform for herself in a contest with an electrifying double. For the duration of the song she would correct the universal rhythm to her own measured swing. Eyes would run over her legs like gold moths brushing at a night pane, to be absorbed into her body – flicker and stare, eyelash and pupil shooting into her bloodstream. The glamour of rehearsing without money in one of Paul's father's barns was an added attraction. We wanted to come at things abrasively, menacingly, casual to the point of being unrehearsed, our minimal accomplishment inimitable in its diffident impact. Our sound would be dissonant, the tight, loaded line delivered with a psychotic, syncopated immediacy, a horneting guitar contesting with an out-of-key barrel-piano.

With green sunlight filtering into the cavernous dark of a stone barn, I read Rubella the new song lyrics that she would appropriate to her voice. There were cows in the meadow, lying down dustily among the cut hay that had been neatly baled for collection. We de-tabbed beer-cans and waited for the first blaze of alcohol to ignite our nerves. Rubella's guitarist was unsociably walled up in himself behind dark shades. His platinum hair curtained his eyes; he wore a white T-shirt slashed with red lipstick welts, his legs poured into black leather trousers. He acknowledged no one; confident of his own virtuoso merits, he played as though Rubella were a supernumerary. The act was natural rather than contrived, the two complementing each other by reason of their mutual hostility. The pianist was an ex-jazz session man, his blue jawed face caved in from the inveterate excesses of a nightclub musician. He gave the appearance of being bewildered by daylight, as though he had been exposed to an element that scoured him. Shielded by dark glasses, a red spotted bandana tied round his forehead, his body attuned to his own unorthodox beat, a rhythm dictated by an idiosyncratic reading of Parker and Coltrane, and an acid-blitzed involvement with sixties psychedelia. Hendrix's fuzzbox having the guitar create its own interpretative locution, a primitive electrification of primal sound, the negroid lips bunching the microphone – 'Purple haze is in my eyes/Excuse me while I kiss this guy'. His hair a purple fuchsia tree, his legs grafted to a peyote cactus.

I read the lyric to Rubella, who followed it on a sheet, and then together we broke it down into a song.

Necrological Bop

When Birdie blew blue Manhattan
out of his cornucopia,
      the improvised cocktail-medley
      incited phallophoria,
a zippy hand on her silk knee
put Damian into ecstasy –
      the red the blue the green the blue
      put leopard spots on what was new
she never knew.

A glitzy sleaze, torch or high camp
is a necrology of those
      who are the candle burning down,
      peeled histrionics of the rose,
a leather hand on the near clown's
little patch of indecency
      was over town all over town
      the red the blue the green the blue
the club came down.

A snarling bop, the singer on his knees
contorted with hysteria,
      invokes the cult of the dead,
      a black snake with a tiara,
he's searching for Jim Morrison
apocalyptic unison –
      the red the blue the green the blue
      elegy to departed stars
who sing on Mars.

   Rubella would strip the lyric to its essential punch-lines, or read it as it stood over a wall of guitar sound. We were aiming to restore the song to a quadruped, to endow it with strong legs, a reference that people could return to rather than live between monosyllabic repetition of chorus lines. We sweated in the red-dark, a tape-recorder picking up the scratchy vocals, the improvised leads cutting out, leaving only a voice and a piano and the pop of exploding beer-cans. Rubella stripped to her black G-string in the furnacing heat, and pared the lyric down similarly.

> When Birdie blew
> blue Manhattan
> the music worked
> on Damian,
> such a cool, blue cool
> leopard-spotted New York,
> such a glitzy sleaze
> by a black swimming-pool.
>
> What will we do
> by a candle and a rose
> when a crazy clown
> runs all over town
> in the blue of the night
> when the music's through
> green and red Manhattan
> I'm in love with you.
>
> Where are they now
> the departed stars
> habitués of the leather bars
> in blue blue Manhattan
> alive with cars
> at 3 a.m.?
> where's Damian
> with Jim Morrison?
> singing on Mars.

The song was cut to a lyric skeleton. It was like a leaf picked clean to its tendrils, fishboned on the petiole. Rubella threw it away with minimal impact, accenting only the unobtrusive images that recurred. In its undoctored form, its rushed impact, it sounded as near to spontaneous impulse as we could achieve. It wasn't success we wanted but shock, the hooking of zany imagery to diametrically opposed rhythm.

We walked back across the blond meadows to the road. It was unreal, this dichotomy between who we were and what we intended to achieve. Light is the great leveller; it exposes us as a toy soldier on the great field of the world. I had not yet acquired an identity. I was too busy trying to apprehend the notion of being here to translate that into quantifiable terms. I was someone becoming someone else, a process that could last all my life.

We were diminutive, heading to a bus-stop with our equipment, Rubella looking unmistakably a star in her tight red skirt and matching lipstick. We spoke about the song and all the others she wished me to write, uncompromising, incandescent lyrics which would encapsulate a novella within the song's four-minute, cheetah-sprung rush. We needed ten songs to impress a record company with the prospect of an album. In our naïvety we imagined that our rough mono-tapes would convey the full impact of our dynamics. Lacking money we assumed that energy would compensate for technique.

We went back to Rubella's flat and sat on a balcony of red geraniums looking out over the rooftops at the marine-blue horizon. Her walls were postered with pin-ups, postcards of Venetian masks, photographs of Bessie Smith and Billie Holliday, the beautiful eyes of Antonin Artaud staring towards a white vision in the skies, a Man Ray photograph of Barbette with black satin lips. Her pantheon of demigods was joined by more immediate influences: David Bowie dressed in sequined leotards or austere with blown-back hair, and the redoubtable angularity of Lou Reed's face, one turned eye negating the world, the other sighting the impossible relationship between a Juan Gris portrait of Picasso and an astronaut mounting a launchpad.

When Dione called round in the early evening, the atmosphere grew tense. His conversation was affected and calculated to disturb. He was derisory of our projected future and spoke only of the need to protect marriage between men and contravene all societal bias towards rigidly defined gender. We were frightened of his vehemence, his spitting intolerance. He was up on cocaine but down in spirits. Something had clearly gone wrong in the course of the day, and Dione who could not accept rejection had clearly been deposed from his pinnacle. He lived in dread of the dead drop from vanity to reality. Having created the artificiality of his person, he feared any visible physical defect that could undermine his simulation of a woman. If someone stared into him, searching not for a flaw but a deeper meaning to his life, he flinched as though found out in the act of committing an unforgivable crime. Tonight he was restive, seeking like an axed snake to knit his body together again, chequered head and tail. We could sense his fangs flickering to punch a venomed incision through our defences. He kept making up, pulling a compact from his pocket and reapplying an orange lipstick, a frosty green eye-shadow. He was inviting attack in order to appease his hurt.

We weren't planning on going anywhere, preferring to sit in the cool of the blue twilight and contemplate our still unearned success. Dione's shadow stained us, inking its way through our porous skins and generating a black chemistry. He was sitting in the one easy chair, a foot trapped beneath his body, his hands held out as though waiting for enamel to dry. 'Let's hit a club, man, and unpocket cash from the elephant's graveyard. Just think of all those snakeskin wallets. One wiggle of the ass and they're yours.'

We ignored him. If he was excluded for long enough he would invariably call a taxi, as he feared the streets at night.

His ideal was to arrive at a club in drag, thereby creating the ultimate mystery as to how he got away with such uncompromising temerity. There were rumours of a chauffeur, a cobalt limousine with shaded windows that disappeared immediately on depositing him at his destination. The lifestyle he dreamt of was translated into a reality by his admirers, and in turn he transposed it into an imaginative reality.

We were anxious to rehearse again, concerned to find lyrics that would stand up on the page as well as find their interpretation through song. I planned to write a sequence about the pressure placed on a singer who couldn't stand up to the imposed stress. Rubella liked the idea of adopting a persona; it was easier to become someone else on stage than to focus on one's own innate traumas. The endless repertoire of songs about unrequited love was what we aimed to avoid, we would present the backstage dilemmas, the person divested of consonantal harmony, the song aimed at being a patched-up catharsis. Our study of lyrics had afforded us an extra dimension; what was relayed beneath the spotlight was most usually a cosmetics kit for clichéd subjectivity. Our dream was to compress the constituents of an elusive novella to the width of a record band.

'You're a bunch of impotent fag-rags,' Dione sneered, his eyes breaking free of their fixed focus and following through to instil terror in us. He got up from his chair, demanding attention by breaking his glass against the wall. We heard the tinkle simultaneous with a glass flower exploding in irregular fragments on the carpet.

Having given voice to his frustration, Dione was left disarmed by his cowardice. He couldn't follow through his dramatic assertion of anger and, fearing reproaches, stormed out into the hall and disappeared. From the balcony we could hear the patter of his pink sneakers. He would be off searching for a taxi, his carnival face too conspicuous to allow for any margin of safety. Most often he avoided trouble by being taken for a girl.

We nursed the cool air, swam in the evening blue of the sky-ceiling and waited for the yellow and black cloud interiors to signal nightfall. We were faces staring into an improbable future; youth looking out of a frieze at a world that disappeared as quickly as a white horse running across the shore at nightfall.

Rubella's evenings were packed with callers. The tiny flat served as a magnet to all those who were drawn by her flamboyant life-style and the excitement that lived in her like a vein of spring water humming to make its dazzling leap into the air. Rubella confided nothing of her private life. She was part Greek, part Portuguese, with vestiges of mulatto blood, her hair alternately black, blonde or red. She had worked as an artist's model, a beautician, a fashion consultant, always living on the fringe of possible careers. Something within her resisted commitment to a single directive; she was like someone who bit at every fruit but tasted none of them. Even now I imagined she would drift off after our initial performance, adopt a new interest with passionate conviction and desert it.

All of us seated in that tiny flat with its red and black hangings, and Nicholas or Paul might drop by to join the company, were in search of an indefinable something which was life itself. An enigma, a theorem, a triangle, whatever it was constituted the reason for consciousness. The dying light broke over our faces like an orange wave. Sitting there, I was already conscious of the big surf that would flood our lives, and how the mind moved from one plane of transition to another, dimension after dimension, nothing to hold one long enough to assume stability. To be in the spotlight's cone is already to be moving out of it. I apprehended how one day one's search would end in a death-room, the little place on earth in which we die. But when I tried to visualize Rubella's death, Dione's, Paul's, Nicholas's, they were all different ones. Would Rubella die as an old woman with dyed blue hair in a little attic in Paris, the concierge left to discover the bunch of red roses she had bought herself as a last celebration of earthly beauty. And Dione? I imagined him overdosing after the hysterical trauma of beating up an older lover who had discovered his infidelity, his habit. He would be found in magenta silk pyjamas, his face painted like a Noh mask. And Nicholas I saw dying with dignity; he would live to be old with a partner, residing in Fiesole, Seville or Aix-en-Provence. His demise would be a quiet one after weeks of anxious consultations. Paul would die surrounded by the oak bedroom furniture that had stood in the farm bedroom for generations. It would be a clear day in February, the cattle making big blue streamers of breath in the meadows, tremulous snowdrops shivering in the woods. His sons would be felling wood in a storm-shattered copse, and only at sundown would they make their way up the wooden stairs, to be met by the family doctor signalling it was all over.

My own death seemed a variant point, something that my life would shape – an endless series of metamorphoses, figurative possibilities, until I found the right state of mind in which to exit. A skylight out of the world. And perhaps one had died many times without the realization that the moment of peace in which we stood looking at a white horse in grey-green grasses in nightfall, or accommodated our minds perfectly to a visual metaphor, was a stopping of life, an unobservance of its physical demands – its insistence that we live by its dictates, and a participation in the timeless interlude that we call death.

As the flat began to fill, so I nurtured the luxury of slipping off alone to the sea. At this hour the bay turned violet and bats frisked the warm sea air. Everything was black, orange and pink. It was like walking into a canvas that extended for the limits of the coast. Strangers would be arriving in the gardens or making their way out to the rocks to swim in the warm night sea. I was searching for something rather than someone, a coloratura that combined word, rhythm, the harmony of being, the pastel interplay of sea and sky colours. I was narrowing in on the elusive arena of the self, touching the magnetic circle that precluded entry, preparing to cross the net of nerve impulses which seemed to have relaxed their warning signals, to have become elastic. The marine night scents, the moths spotting the enfiladed pink lilies, the light in the waves' overhang that was grainy like shredded coconut, everything contrived to create the effect of a luminous synaesthesia, an orchestration of the senses which uplifted me. I was moon-walking; there appeared to be no distance between the nearest star and the stone steps leading to the garden, when I was jolted out of this state of trance by a hand placed squarely on my shoulder. I swung round to find a girl looking at me. Her green eyes and heart-shaped face with its carnation lips was taut with the need to impart a message before the person cut off behind that need could flood through.

'I know what it is,' she said, before her smile broke and she ran back down the promenade, a barefooted, tight-jeaned figure with black hair slipping into the lavender dusk come off the sea.

There wasn't anyone else around. I slipped into the garden with her words trapped inside me. That single phrase had come to constitute a lexicon. The night had come on in perfect stillness. I propped myself up and watched the lit decks of a passenger ship crawl slowly across the skyline. You could be somewhere else just by following a moving object: a displacement had occurred. I was already someone else.

Part Two

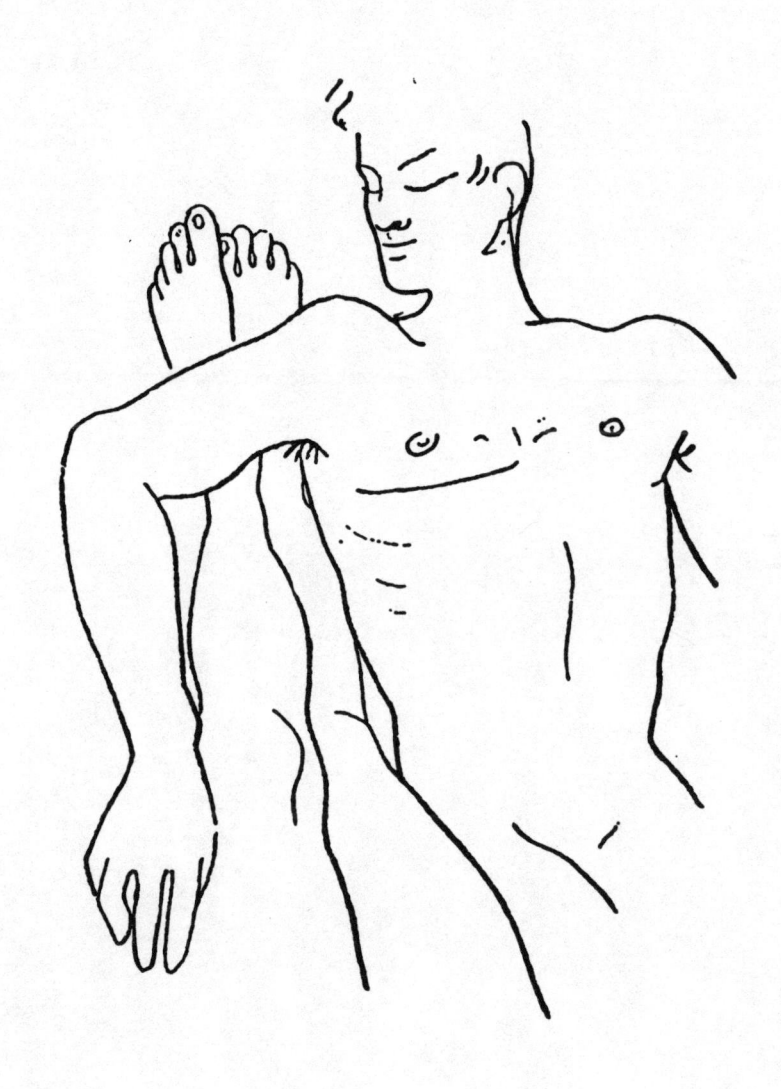

Chapter 4

Dione lit a pink cocktail cigarette and drew on the gold filter tentatively, not wishing to smudge his lipstick. His diamond bracelet lit up with an affected down-turn of his wrist. Time was running out on us, three more weeks and our summer would end – the green leaf would acquire gold speckles and finally break free as a scarlet canoe charting the blue skies.

The tension told in us; we were flying by standing still. Nicholas was morose, fidgety, moody at the prospect of the disbanding of our fraternity. Paul seemed reconciled to the prospect of the future. For him it would always comprise a dichotomy, a hairline flaw in an otherwise unquestioned character. We stood in the gold shimmer of the afternoon, the air standing still, the heat trapping us like a net. Something had to happen. A green sea vitrified in the cove.

'I'm free now,' Dione said. 'I've written to my parents.

Education is a thing of the past. I'm going to be taken care of.'

I could see the sadness darken Paul's face like a bay filling with cloud shadows. Something told him he would never see Dione again, that their lives would follow such different ways that he had only these few weeks to make an impression, of which he knew himself to be incapable. He would remember this all his life – the mulberry tree in the garden, his confusion, the risk he incurred by participating in our clandestine meetings, the open-ended sentence of his life over which hovered an enigmatic, sunlit question mark.

Dione wanted to push us into his terrapin-bowl of contenders. 'You don't know what real kicks are,' he would say. 'The parties I go to are unrestrained. The rich cruisers that snort, have got access to a mint. They can place you anywhere across the globe.'

He stopped speaking and drew on his pink cigarette. His black silk top moulded itself to the guitar-neck of his slim body. He wasn't really here at all, drugs had placed him in an illusory state. He was still living out one of the innumerable parties he attended where men danced in stilettos and tight skirts and trebled, quadrupled on panther-skins in the master bedroom. But he paid the price of bitterness for his bargaining promiscuity. The cashmere jumpers, Hermes scarves, monogrammed cigarette-cases, all of these gifts were gasconaded in exchange for flesh. And Dione took them in excess; they were the triumphant symbols of inversion sold on the hard scaffold block of the bed.

'There's a party at Max's tonight,' he said. 'The way to the top lies in meeting people. None of you have the courage to break with your fears. To really let go, one's got to risk everything. . . .'

No one answered. There was a broodiness amongst us, a touch-paper crackle of frayed nerves. The summer had been too long and too wearying; the heat was sealed in us like wine in a corked bottle – a red fire that had still to mellow.

Someone's temper had to flare like a luminous Spanish firework.

I wanted to walk off to the rocks and be done with Dione. I could see Nicholas skirting the edges of any confrontation, picking at loose threads in his mind, tidying up corners as a distraction from Dione's incursion on privacy. Paul was withdrawn into his own solid acres. He must have been shaken by the feminine within him, that loop in the thread that denied him unification with his inherited world. Even helping his father with the potato crop, body straining in the furrow after the digger, hands blackened from loose topsoil, he was denied the completion that would have integrated him with a community. He must have known that one day his father would come up the stairs for him with lumbering deliberate strides, and then stand in the doorway, mouth ajar, not even knowing how to speak of the gravity of something of which he himself was ignorant.

'I might even turn you lot in to your parents,' Dione said, feeding the inner monster within him. 'You don't know what I'm capable of doing. If you think you're protected by a fraternity, you're wrong. I'm the one who's free. The rest of you are dependent on my tolerating you.'

At times like these one could feel the towering rage in Dione rise like a sudden squall at sea. It was the shadow in him, the omnivorous chimera achieving ascendancy that drove him into a blood-stained alley from which he pelted those near to him with stones. He demanded adulation for the imagined god within him. Denied that, he became a black narcissus – an implacable junkie dusted with cocaine and sparkling facepowder. 'I'll stick a dude one of these nights,' he said with the bitter, avenging tone of someone who has been rejected.

Nicholas began to walk off slowly. He was trying to defuse the situation by simulating absorption in the two or three figures below us on the beach. He leant against the ivied wall and stared out at the wind-lifted blue blouse of the bay. Paul was so sunk into himself that he might have been the knagged trunk of the mulberry that spread its shade over us. We were all solidifying into objects separate from Dione. His words couldn't reach us; soon we would be metamorphosed into stone, tree, mineral, light.

One by one we slipped off, tentatively. The heat, the blue air, the dazzle of light refracted from the bay had us look back at the garden as though it was an oasis suspended between two shores, two reaches of sky. Only when we were out of sight did we regroup, fearing all the while that Dione would see our defection as conspiratorial. We walked out to the nearest of the inshore reefs, a loaf-shaped rock tufted with marram and sea-pinks, and calligraphized with orange lichen. By slipping into a blind-side gully we could be concealed from the shore. A man came out of the water, his body still sheathed in the glaze of salt, a blue film that clung to him as he tented himself in an orange beach-towel.

No one wanted to speak; we stood there, together and apart. Each of us knew it was an end to our life with Dione. He was swinging out on a trajectory that would have him plummet into the void. He would end up crazed, vicious, an oiled body strung out on the rack. We had already heard of how he had taken to calling himself Marilyn and to fluffing up his skirt at drag parties. His face was grey chalk beneath the cosmetics, a draughtsman's sketch to be fleshed out with angle and plane. And we knew too that, once turned against us, his reprisals would be unsparing. His avenging machinations were knotted in his stomach like a spider's compacted silk. He would line us in with viscous reticulations, jerking the thread tighter until we were drawn face up to his black eye. He was capable of writing anonymous letters to our parents, and worse still of humiliating us in public. All of the abuse, the objurgation directed at his person had instilled in him a loathing for those of his own kind. Self-hate was bottled in him like black acid. When he could direct the siphon at someone similarly vulnerable, he delighted to watch the acid scald.

We could feel the hollow open up in our lives. We had risked a trust too early; our words, our actions, our involvements with this place were implanted in Dione. We were all of us in his head – we lived there independent of ourselves and as autonomous satellites of his mind. Fiction began at the point of speech. An admission, an illumination of the self, was the qualifying exchange for endless variants. Words were seeds that planted metaphoric forests.

Nicholas took his clothes off and slipped into the green jasper of a gully that extended like a narrow beak to the bay. Paul was troubled; I could see his thoughts sink like pebbles thrown into a clear pool.

'Two more weeks and he has to go and kill it for us. It's crazy. Why did we ever start coming here?'

There was no answer; only the leisurely lip of the wave as it rose towards our feet lifting the sea-bed with it, so that a Persian carpet of maroons, modenas and cobalts appeared to tilt upward to the surface. Nicholas was a head on a glass platter. A group of men dived by him playfully, but he came out of the water and sat alone on the point looking out to the skyline. If a camera had then closed on the scene, isolating in black and white the moment of his being there, the evocation of solitude would have come closer to thought itself, the particular distinguished from the general, the thought identifying itself with the seascape, crystallizing around the sea's translucency.

Paul took a packet of crumpled Lucky Strikes from his pocket and the fragrant smoke smelt of summer, sun-tan oil, lavender bags placed in drawers. Ruminative, hunched into himself, he seemed to want to come clear of his way of life. He might have been sitting on a grain-sack, shifting his weight in order to hear the seed-heads crunch like the sound of scuffed gravel.

The sea was beginning to involve us in its rhythm. If one were to let go, one would be sucked into the tide without resistance. The incoming and the retreating wave established no opposition in this calm. The hanging smoke from Paul's cigarette combined to create a narcotic effect that dulled our alertness to time. The sound of the wave swung us in a phosphorescent hammock. We had forgotten all about Nicholas out there on a spine of rock. He was blue on blue, green on green, someone who had turned invisible in the light.

When the shout went up it was explosive. We didn't know what it was or why it meant Nicholas, and someone was already dressed and running back to the shore to raise the alarm. Fear was dynamiting its way through our consciousness. The idea that it could be Nicholas who was in trouble gagged in my throat. Fear electrified my nerves. The silence was terrible. The sky was beginning to jump in cinematic cut-ups. I thought of Nicholas's small head attached to an expanding balloon of water, his body huge, inflatable and slowly being pulled away from his head which fought to remain on the surface. He was powerless. The inner scream couldn't cut through water. We were suddenly divided from him by an inner and outer reality. It was as though the earth we stood on was no longer tangible. Everything we had come to believe or take for granted was being detonated. In a livid, hallucinated flash I could see my parents standing on a bridge in the sky, looking down at the bay. They were both younger than I had known them; my father's hair was blond and inexplicably he was wearing a Nazi uniform.

A crowd had gathered on the gully-point. Men were shielding their eyes from the glare, straining to find the image they had already mentally formed of a head fighting to keep above the water-line. For the first time I was faced with the realization of the immensity of the universe. I was powerless. The radius of my arms was infinitesimal against the horizon. It was only my mind that could centre things. I could bring

Nicholas into my head without having to locate him in physical space. I thought of him hooked by the current's tentacles. Time had become water. Was it a minute or an hour ago that I had looked up to see him sitting there on the rock, the water flashing like peridots on his back? He hadn't the time to get out in the middle of the bay with nothing between him and the sky. I knew from swimming here that the current was like an eel, winding its coils and squeezing with cold, sustained pressure. It could turn a man blue and swallow him.

Everything I knew about Nicholas lit up in my mind. I could see him in every aspect I knew of him, his face huge and demanding, contracted and disappointed, the terror in his eyes in the moment of truth that he was falling down a flight of stone stairs, his quiet sense of well-being when reading a book, and now his agony framed in the rictus of a scream. I kept telling myself that this couldn't be real. The scene that was stuck in my head would revert to an image of safety. If I thought hard enough my intentions would materialize.

Paul seemed to have turned to stone. Everyone was watching a swimmer who had gone out, his powerful, crisp strokes cutting through the water with the streamlined reach of a dolphin. Nicholas's life was somehow inextricably linked to this stranger's. He had become the focal point of hope. As long as this man existed, so too was there hope of Nicholas's survival. I seemed to be standing outside of time, isolated from the event by my refusal to believe it was happening. And then it was starting up: the intrusion of a mewling klaxon. It was like a white apparition that had materialized out of nowhere, the ambulance parked on the slip, while the fire-brigade launched their zippy emergency craft, a high-powered, inflatable dinghy that would bounce across the inshore calm.

It was impossible to believe that all this was happening for Nicholas. The wasp buzzing at my shoulder was loud as an outboard. People stood looking out to sea, but there wasn't anything to observe, only the glare hitting in, and the steady filling of the gullies with deep blue water. The sea had become Nicholas's body, it was his flailing arms which set up the beat of waves.

The swimmer came back to the rocks, exhausted, breathing hard like a man who has pitched himself against a wall. He had touched the peripheral undercurrent and sprung back from the force of shock. He was getting his words out between painful respiration. 'It's impossible, the current almost had me.' Friends were wrapping him in towels, for, despite the heat, he had struck cold depths. He was shaking, enervated by the unreality, exhausted from the urgency of his bid; a man delivered by the tide to a cradling support of arms.

We watched the launch head out and swing round in a slow, increasing circle. We had imagined it would be up close, a fixture of the inshore, but we heard its motor making for deeper water, churning, then accelerating in abrupt spasms. Each time the speed decreased we envisaged Nicholas being pulled on board, only to hear the buzzing resume, the throttle opened with an urgent injection of fuel.

By now people were gathering on the beach, alert to a crisis in which they felt themselves indirectly involved. They were trying to grasp what was happening on a psychic plane, learning by empathic fractions to understand their mortality. Whatever was out there was as much an abstraction as the idea of death. It was a sunspot, a visual point of reference, an identification of their fear for which they were searching. They had been called out of an ordinary afternoon to be confronted with the crisis. Some had emerged from the cover of sleep, others had sensed a growing disquietude dilate like a black cloud crossing the sun. Only the shadow wouldn't disperse. No one could get access to what had occurred; they couldn't pull their drift tight to a locatable centre.

We listened to the boat's intermittent findings, but always the speed was taken up again, the search renewed. People were down at the sea's edge, hands shading their eyes, gathered there like an exodus of creatures pushed to flight by news of an invisible enemy advancing behind them.

The heat was walling into us despite the off-glance of wind from the sea. We too were being forced back by the incoming tide; we had to climb up to a higher vantage-point while the sea deepened perceptibly. I could see a green crab shifting sideways over stones picked out in the champagne colour of the shallows. It moved at a tilting pace, now brushing through brown weed, now scuttling across blue stones. It was a potentate of the underfloor, its stalked eyes raised from a camouflaged carapace.

We were left alone. A stream of urine was trickling down Paul's leg; he was involuntarily shaking. Those who knew of our connection with Nicholas stood off, testing the air, unwilling to intrude on our air-sealed precinct. We were under glass, helmeted by isolation. We would be faced with the problem of explaining his and our presence here. The past beat at my face with a leather strap. In my imagination Nicholas was blue ice, but a red mouth had opened in the ice-mask, an oval expressive of unmediated pain. It was then that I knew he was dead. He might already have made the journey somewhere else. He would be trying to reach us, only we couldn't hear. The jet of urine dried into the warm surface of the rock on which Paul was standing. I wanted to scream, but I feared losing my sanity.

It was the limitless nature of the sea that was suddenly impressed on us. And when we looked out, distance translated itself into depth, the void became a psychophysical phenomenon, a gulf in which to implode and a savage death-trap that had swallowed Nicholas. The sea we looked at was a luminous belly in which the drowned circulated on the arm of the current before being dragged over rocks, mutilated by the thrashing swell.

Nothing would stabilize. The pieces in my mind fragmented

and wouldn't reconnect. I could taste blood in the back of my nose; my heart was beating with hammer-blows. As I stood there I could see all of us as we had been before the catastrophe. Dione in a mellower, less-drugged state, his feminine charm unadulterated by bitchy acerbity, the blue smoke-rings escaping from his pink mouth. Nicholas, discreet, generous about life, careful never to overstep the limitations in which he felt comfortable, speaking of his future as though it were settled, and how his father's money would assist him in whatever undertaking he wished. His mind lived with the security of an indefinite latitude. Time would wait for him; at a given moment he would decide on his role in life and the thing would be effortlessly consummated. And Paul, I saw him at his least strained, amiable, his big arms loose at his side, speaking of the land, the cycle of crops, and how no one need ever come to know of his difference. There would be his wife and innumerable male lovers met under cover of dark. When the mind was at rest, a dual future was possible. But now, at the motivation of a single involuntary act, all our futures were spun into irregular orbits. We were standing on a narrow bridge; the planks behind and in front of us had collapsed; and the immediate hurt by coming too close, and was pushing its unavoidable prospect at us with the force of a stick wedged between teeth.

There were two launches working the tide. They went out on an approximate clockwise and anti-clockwise circumference, intersecting at a given point on the blue hub.

The ferocity of the present built in me until I wanted to retch. I kept on wondering where and what there was to go back to. Interrogation, family scenes, the inference that we had all in part contributed to Nicholas's death by associating with an area of the beach which we were strictly forbidden to visit. There was too much time left in the day, and tomorrow the vacuum would increase. If I tried to think of the future it was like staring into a cone of light which was blocked at one end. Nicholas was a water balloon. If ever we accepted the idea of his death, we would think of him intensely at first, then later on he would become an abstraction, a Nicholas who would return with intermittent, blinding clarity as though to reproach us for our neglect of him. But the going back would be like walking barefoot over splintered glass. There would be parents, friends, a school to face. All of them would demand that we somehow bring Nicholas out of hiding. Our lives would be connected with the mystery of his death. There would be too much of us and too little of him.

'Let's get out of here,' Paul insisted, his voice breaking into desperation. 'We've got to find Dione.'

As we stood there, the tide at our heels, playfully warm in the shallows, it was as if we were petrified, our hands and feet breaking free of stone. We had known fear transmogrify us into lithic statues. There was nothing we could do but run away from the impossible. A crowd had gathered round the semicircular bay, all of them awaiting some momentous event to occur. Everyone was facing outwards as though fixated by the notion of a pineapple-sized skull becoming suddenly visible on the surface.

We ran back, trying not to draw attention to ourselves, but unable to contain our desperation. The air was suddenly cool on my spine as though we had crossed from summer to winter without knowing of the change.

We came up off the beach as if hunted. Paul's feet were cut from fragments of glass. We felt we were being spotlighted as we made our way back up the stone steps to our garden refuge. Dione had gone. The place was altered in some way, the bench half in shade and half in light, while a solitary bee crackled in the dark ivy lockets. We felt as though we were being repulsed by the one refuge we had come to recognize as home. We weren't wanted here any longer. The stone walls tried to beat us off. The mulberry told the season with its necklace of red stains blotching the ground. The whole place was taking on the burden of history; it was participating in becoming a cameo in time. These wind-warped oaks, this rugged mulberry, the beds of twinkling scarlet and white petunias, the pink lilies with their vase-like calyxes, all these were somehow involved in our change. They and we had come this far in a certain relationship, a way of seeing and interacting that led to a reciprocal sensitization – eye and thing – the mutual realization of a harmony established by interplay. We stood there shaking. Something outside of our control had involved us in its inexorable course. Nicholas was drowning inside me. I could feel him depriving me of strength. I was standing on air, fighting for breath, watching Paul's features develop into a blur.

We were trapped. We felt too frightened to move, and at the same time confident that, if only we found Dione, things would somehow come right. We couldn't think: we threw ourselves against mirrors which in turn magnified our fear. If only Dione knew what had happened, he might effect a reversal, a restoration of the drowned man. There were eyes everywhere; people had gathered higher up in the garden in order to watch the zigzag radiuses of the rescue launches. They were still buzzing inshore and then describing sweeping arcs until they became inaudible specks in the marine light.

It was coming up to the time when we were both expected home from the beach. One of us would have to call and break the news and listen to the shock run like a tidal wave down the wires to connect at the other end. The electrocuting bolt would press home to an hysterical reception. 'Where, how and why?' We were the potentially classifiable irresponsibles who would be held culpable for Nicholas's death.

We got dressed, feeling for clothes that seemed elusive to the fingers. This slow-motion ritual was like the preparation for an act of great significance. In the living out of each moment of terror, I knew that we would never forget it: the light, the garden, our powerlessness to act. I could feel the day turn black and stand above me with its threatening overhang. It wasn't my voice I heard, coming from a long way away. 'Let's find Dione,' I said. 'It can't be Nicholas. It fucking well can't be.'

Paul was moon-faced, bent double with a shoe. 'We're still assuming it's him. What if he got bored, and went off with Dione, without our knowing it. There's always a chance.'

His words resonated hollowly. I kept thinking that if only language could alter time, upend the ontological construct of being, and substitute in its place an orphic enlivening, so that to articulate a word was to bring about the corresponding change in the universe, then the voice of poetry would have succeeded. My consciousness was awakening to a deeper form of lyric; the pop song was only a scratch on the surface – an abbreviated street-slang. A new voice was coming clear, a note from deeper strata...

'Quick, let's get away from here.' Paul importuned. His face was splashed with tears. The sun was the light amber of acacia honey as we made for the road to the town. We took a short cut down a looping hill which overlooked the harbours and beyond that the bay. Small fishing-craft were constellated across the blue expanse – lobster dorys, dinghies, the brightly coloured sails of yachts.

We walked in step, recognizing nothing. Buildings were abstracted, blank cubes and rectangles broken up into planes that resembled Franz Marc's depiction of Tyrol. We gained on the town without being concious of our steps eating up the road. We were just there, hitting into narrow side-streets that gave on to a central square, its bronze Victor Hugo raised on a pediment limed by guano. We had to follow up a back alley to arrive at the Blue Mink. The skull-shaven doorman, dressed in black leather with two hooped piratical earrings, admitted us into a bar illuminated by red and silver spotlights. The black walls were a photomontage of glamorous stars: Louise Brooks, Barbette, Dusty Springfield,

Coco Chanel, satin lipstick bows and eyes darkened like black lakes.

Dione was standing amongst a ruck of admirers. He was wearing a red fez for affectation. A blue-haired man was kissing his right ear-lobe and playfully lipping an earring that sparkled like a firefly, a topaz elongation of his ear. Curlicues of blue smoke snaked to the ceiling. Dione was holding two glasses, his unsteady hands balancing them as in a juggler's act. He was being fêted on all sides.

'Hey sugar, take a walk on the wild side,' struck up the familiar Lou Reed chorus line.

> But she never once lost her head
> Even when she was giving the greatest head.
> Hey man, take a walk on the wild side.

Paul moved directly towards Dione. His peremptory manner had the sycophantic swarm of neophytes part to right and left of their drunken queen.

'Dione, you've got to get out of here,' Paul said. 'It's Nicholas. He's drowned off the rocks. We've just come from the beach. They're still looking for him. Quickly, you've got to help us...'

People were tugging at Paul's shirt. They didn't want him there. Dione was wavering between the euphoric fog of his high and the words that snapped at him like a leather strap laid across the face. He was anaesthetized against shock; the words came back off his consciousness like a ball rebounding from a brick wall. He opened his mouth in the fish-oval of a stupefied smile. He wasn't able to connect with Paul's electrifying urgency.

'Don't you understand,' Paul was shouting. 'Nicholas is dead, you stupid bastard!'

Dione fumbled to articulate. Words struggled to come to the surface but stayed down. When they tried to emerge, their order was confused, incoherent, disconnected from the mains. Two hands were locked around Dione's waist supporting him from behind, while lips kissed his shoulders. He leant back into his cushioning partner. He was like a woman being courted before love.

There wasn't anything we could do. We left the bar abruptly, letting the wooden door bang on its hinges. Outside, there was still the same sunlight, the same street with its pedestrian traffic. I tried to convince myself that none of this was real and that we would go back to the beach to find the crowds dispersed, the high tide lipping the sea-wall and Nicholas standing with his arms crossed, preparing to go home.

We set off without direction. We couldn't go back to the shore, we were too deeply implicated in a death to trust in our not being apprehended. Dimension and perspective had changed, it was no longer the same town we walked through – the buildings were too close, glazed with an onyx light, people resembling figures snowing across the backdrop of a cinema screen.

We were moving without seeing, and once Paul rebounded off an angular shoulder and for a split second his mind connected with reality. Fear blazed through him with a jolting electricity. We were like figures caught up in the diaspora after Babel. There was no longer a language in which to communicate our contained hysteria. When I thought of the beach I imagined it black with crows – an ink storm of birds convening by the sapphire waters, Nicholas's blue body wrapped like a mummy in white bandages.

We struck out towards the edges of the town. The evening crowds were going home under the copper-red sun. Cars sat in a bowl of petroleum vapour, edging forward tail to tail before making for the coast, surf-boards attached to roof-racks. They were making for the ocean. We pointed forwards, the crisis belling in our faces. There wasn't anywhere to go; we just had to keep walking, as though by doing so we could overtake our pain. We came out to a wasteland swathed with thistle-down. The rusted chassis of a car was submerged in a green sea of nettles. We got into the patch and collapsed, exhausted. We were safe here from having to own up to others. Paul lay out flat like someone winded and recovering from shock. There were butterflies twinkling on the thistles – red admirals, cabbage whites – and swarms of burnet moths. On the other side was a garden orchard; its green apples touched with brickish red looked sharp, ciderish, acidic in the russet sun.

We were somewhere we had never thought to visit; a weird twist of the spiral had deposited us here amongst the junked ephemera left to the slow erosion of the elements. We would have to go back and face the antagonistic incredulity of parents. Their interrogation would be another form of drowning, a remorseless sinking in of words that would touch bottom and stay there like sand-weighted wrecks on the sea-floor. The wrong words were like anchors and left biting indentations in the psyche.

'My father will kill me,' Paul said. And I imagined a knotted giant of a man twisted with rage come in from the fields to hold measure over his son with a stout stick. In his mind the land would have been betrayed, his son's imagined iron fist vitiated to a flower stem.

When I thought of my own parents my mind went blank. Their faces were suddenly abstracted to moons. They were blanks floating in the void – Mr and Mrs Moon. Their method of coping with the situation would be to avoid me. I would be confined to my room and left to familiarize myself with the blue wallpaper, the insulating silence. I would read Rimbaud and write my own hallucinated poetry. Solitude was like being trapped inside a jewel. No one could reach in, but one faced out into a universal association of images.

Paul got up and searched along the near-side wall, his hands buried deep in his pockets. I kept hearing a voice that never quite reached us but fell short in a series of muffled echoes. It wasn't Nicholas's, it was modified into the impersonally cosmic. Paul was poking in the grass with his eye, looking for anything that would offer a point of focus, a clue, a stability. Buckled cobalt bottle-caps, rusted cans, a metallic tiger-beetle tilted across a leaf, the invisible shadow of his thoughts casting penumbral colours on the sun-washed clover. There had to be something small, insignificant and neglected that would answer to being the resonant symbol which would provide a meaning to his inner chaos.

He came back towards where I was sitting on a log snaked with ivy. His legs were rigid, his head followed his feet as through he were concentrating on bouncing a slow ball. 'I'm terrified,' he said. 'Let's get away from here. I'm sure someone's watching us. Let's go back to the sea. It's our only hope.'

We could still hear the helicopter's persistent reverberations. It was audible like a loud bee confined to an echo-chamber. Its bulbous dragonfly's head was trained down as it picked up on its reconnaissance.

There was something terrible about Paul's expression and face. He appeared to be crying inwardly without any show of tears. I could see his nerves disintegrating. We were two creatures shocked into non-being. Ghosts of the sunlight, we had been blown so far back from our centres that we sleep-walked through our motions. Something had to break. I could feel the energy in Paul rising to a detonative head. When we got to the bottom of a steep gradient which connected with the outskirts of the town he took off at a breakneck pace. He was jumping cars, zigzagging the traffic, his white shirt billowing behind him in the suffocating evening heat. I didn't attempt to stay with him. He was running crazily, levering himself off stationary bonnets, and was soon out of sight, looping the corner and gone.

Chapter 5

When I looked up, the walls and ceiling were painted blue with a white dividing border. I seemed to breathe out and return to an emptiness – the hollow sensation that Nicholas was irretrievably gone. It was like falling off a roof in a dream, to find oneself indefinitely suspended before the jolt. Nicholas's body had been found by offshore fishermen. It had been dragged out by the rip-tide into mid-channel.

I spent hours trying to envisage what he looked like dead. Abstractions swam into my mind. The blotched blues and purples of a jellyfish, his body blown up tumescent from water, seal-heavy, powdered with bruises and aubergine abrasions. And at other times he was featureless, his skin pearl-blue and his face erased like ink in water. There was nothing to distinguish him as Nicholas other than my imagining him so and investing the symbol with his name and characteristics. He appeared to me as the stream of consciousness directed – sometimes as he was, fastidious, his black cashmere jumper sitting perfectly on his shoulders, a peridot emphasizing the little finger of his left hand. At other times he was floating composed on the surface of the water, his head tilted back above the waves, his eyes black with kohl, his mouth open in an ambiguous smile.

I lay face down and watched the hallucinations implode across inner space. Dione, Nicholas, Paul – whatever had impressed in our summers together came back with renewed intensity. The past was combusting with the roar of a bonfire. Faces poked through orange and red roses. Dione's sneering lips opening to a lipsticked pout to entice a banker, Paul's uneasy eyes expressing fear of his involvement with our group. Nicholas secure in the assurance of his future, my excitement at the prospect of Rubella singing my lyrics. Red and white starlights chasing across a black stage.

The visuals changed and rearranged themselves according to the degree of my concentration. The house was too quiet; it was as though my parents had moved out, leaving me the abandoned occupant of a silent floor. Footsteps approached on muffled feet down the parquet corridor. They seemed to hang fire outside my room before going about their business elsewhere. I was forgotten; a body confined to a blue hypogeum. When they broke into my airless chamber and unwound me from white sheets, I would dematerialize. They would try hard to remember my features in the way that Nicholas's parents must have been distraught at losing the exact photographic memory of how their son looked at home, at school, in the last holidays. Only in dream would a likeness recur, and on waking they would struggle to keep the image, only to let it go in the hope of relinquishing a disturbance, a fish too powerful for their daylight lives and one which would pull them back into the night waters in which they had seen a terrifying underwater vision. And Nicholas would keep returning to them, phosphorescent, meteoric, a face sometimes appealing for help, and at other times so luminously serene that they would wake thinking he was still alive.

I was conscious too of the end of our summer. Valuable days were being eroded, and the freedom we had imagined as breaking over us in these last pre-equinoctial days, the jasper wave pushing us clear into an unobstructed future, was now an undercurrent paralysing us with its coldness. I thought of Paul similarly winded in a cool pool, trapped there until the returning tide established a new high-water mark. And Dione already capitalizing on having known Nicholas. In his world casualties were expected – the jilted lover overdosing in a bedroom on a counterpane splashed with Sardinian lilies, the masochist tied up while rent boys inflicted knife-wounds on his skin, the man dying eventually when the thing worked itself into a frenzy, the pain he identified with an initiation into death finally opening out into a blood rose. Dione was fascinated by death and the legends of those who had died young. He saw himself as one of the inevitable early dead – the young man with a red heart tattoed on his nape and a rose on his bottom found in silk sheets after weeks of excess. His name would be propagated as a myth in the white afternoon sunlight. There would be rumours of a scandalous death-note penned in blood with the promise of a return. A black-eyed face laughing in an alley, a figure seen walking across the sands at noon, a voice echoing through the misty gullies.

In the confinement of my room I began to invent fictions that were realities. I was withdrawn into a microcosm that permitted no intruders. Our summer beach lived inside my head like a ship in a bottle. I spent hours in that mental landscape given over to the autonomy of unconscious travel. At intervals I would write up my findings and attempt to commit them to the page with the same hallucinatory colour and intensity as they appeared to me through the view-finder of the imagination. The difficulty was always in getting words to conform to the cinematic speed of visual stills.

My parents were determined to keep me in for a week. As I lay there it seemed like the denial of a lifetime, as though my eyes and mouth were full of sand and my senses insulated from their spontaneous impulses. I would miss Rubella's performance of my songs and the see-through black skirt she intended to wear on stage. The chance had gone wide of me, she would move on and find new acquaintances, self-pen her lyrics in a late-night bar and let the whole act go at the first failure.

If the telephone rang in the house it was answered summarily. I had become non-existent to the outside world. I too was drowning, in the blue room, watching my life replay itself in a series of fulminating exposures. I was opening windows that revealed the universe: red starfish, blue mussels, triton and conch, stars that had burnt out in their meteoric exits. If I pushed on through far enough, I would encounter Nicholas and the great mysteries, love and death.

I was permitted the use of my radio and books. Exhausted from inner exploration and the consumption of psychic energy, I would tune into fast music and have it flood my nerves. I wanted to regain contact with Paul. I imagined life must be terrible for him, the stolid incomprehension of parents, the guilt attendant on being blamed for something in which one played an indefinable role – all of these things must have welled up to a concentrated dark. I imagined him out in woods behind the farm, moody, brooding in the heart of a clearing, sitting astride a rotten log, the underside of which supported a colony of wood-lice. Long days of being alone with himself and returning to the farm kitchen for meals and to hear his father's indefatigable monologue on how the price of potatoes was down again. There would be the smell of musty sunlight, barn straw, the incipient putrefaction of the season's first pheasant hung up to rot until it fell. I had sat in Paul's kitchen on such late summer afternoons, hearing his mother employ a Brittany patois unintelligible to all but those in her parish. Paul accepted it as a first language until, his sophistication increasing, he had come to despise this hybrid vernacular. Now it must have grated with its implications of a parochial retrogression, that sealed, incestuous world of intermarriage for the propagation of the land. The stiff ceremonial marriages, loveless and acquisitive, the guests drawn away from the churches in black limousines that could have been hearses. In the slow-motion scenario I was condemned to watch, faces came up close, hypnotizing one into the same terror induced by a pike on a small fish as it basks on the surface of a pond before returning to its depths. Paul's father with his beetroot cheeks and expressionless brown eyes kept bumping up against my mental camera. Then it was his mother, stooped, prematurely old at fifty, her horizons contracted to a stone kitchen where neighbours called to impart gossip and contrive those same marriages that sealed a rural community into a feudal compress of clay.

Paul must have lain in bed at night and felt the earth cover him – his legs, waist, arms, the clay spreading to his neck and solidifying into a parched crust. On awakening he would have to cut himself out of a sheet of stiff earth. He would rise with his ancestral terrain moulded to him as though he was a seed potato putting out farinaceous tubers. I remembered days spent in the ciderish apple orchard, colts frisking farther down the meadow, the apples tanning to a red-streaked russet, our first tart mouthfuls spiking the tongue, sweet, acidic, sharp, all blended in the spurt of juice come from the crisp pulp. We would pelt each other with the crop like snowballs. Unripe apples smashed open against granite walls. We took horse-bites into green rondures and recoiled. Nicholas would come there too, but never Dione. Nicholas would sit quietly under a tree and watch the horses move into blue areas of shade. A white stallion and a chestnut mare, they choreographed a valley meadow along which a stream twisted in its journey through bulrushes.

It was apple time again, only none of us would make light of the dappled fruit; windfalls would thud into the grasses, bruised by their own penumbral exits. The young boy from a neighbouring cottage would sit hour after hour floating his red-sailed toy yacht in the cow-pond. Sitting out there one could make believe there wasn't a world of time involving active participation in its schema. There was only air, our still undiscovered futures, the swallow's frenetic dip for horse-flies, the silent pacing of cloud shadows across the grass. In that stillness I could remember Paul gauchely lighting a cigarette in an attempt to puff up his ego. Blue curlicues of smoke fogged out the sun-faced dandelion.

I could have been there now if it weren't for the weird shift of time that had elapsed between our seeing Nicholas broken up by planes of sunlight, sitting out on a rock, already removed from us and the blinding recognition that he had gone out to sea before we could ever think of him again. Somewhere in that interval was the amnesiac pivot that had drifted wide of its centre, causing us to forget. It was for that act of involuntary blindness that I was now confined to the rigours of parental discipline. It was that which separated me from the cool meadow grass at Paul's farm, the circle that Rubella and Dione kept. I imagined the latter now standing in the doorway to someone's kitchen, his mouth full of hairpins, casually dismissing death, anyone's death, as a necessary error. Rubella would be humming a song, rhythmically floating her hips to the beat. She didn't need Dione, whose insidious affectation infiltrated into all those who believed that by knowing him they would establish contacts indispensable to their future. Dione was a hollow bamboo, a vessel of empty expectations. His promise couldn't be faulted, for it was others who read into his flawed character the unity of their own lives. Nothing could touch Dione: he remained impervious to others. His ideal would have been to discover that people were no different from the wooden figures in a shooting-gallery, only that in blowing off their heads they divulged money, jewels, air tickets to Caribbean resorts.

Day swam into night like the blue current in a grotto turning green and finally black. A nerve flexed in my body when the radio picked up on Lou Reed's voice, his understated, perfectly placed syllables reaching the chemistry that snowed goose-pimples on one's skin.

> And a pretty face can have its way
> But to tramps like us we were born that way.

We had all been born that way, but there were variations of the spiral's twist, loops and quirks that allowed for an extensible ambivalence. What I imagined was a ladder telescoping into the sky with irregular rungs, some of them punched out, others eroded by rust, the shape of the ladder forming a serpent in the heavens, a colubrine bent that ended in the flickering of a gold-fanged star.

The wind blew up on the fourth night of my confinement to the house. I could hear the breakers growling in the bay and their pebble-mouthed snarl lift with the wind. It was the first outbreak of storm all summer, and I lay listening to the confusion of elements, a black swollen tide lift towards the brutal stars. It was the first premonitory gesture of the equinox, that insurgent roar of green waters which would batter the coast, while the wind stripped the vine and shook out a banner of red leaves.

My past rose with the wind; it came at me in a slow-motion procession like a hand endlessly revealing cards. Facets, vignettes, states of being, incidents partially or fully recorded, things lodged in the memory and freed by a psychic upheaval, the whole eruptive core flew into identifiable fragments. A branch trailed against the window, its firm whiplash trying the glass. Something within me was feeling out spaces I had still to explore. Words lived in there and the discovery of them evoked a corresponding symbol. I started to write down my findings, sheltering the page from an imagined reader over my shoulder. At the slightest notion of a footstep I sprang up to defend my inner terrain. This gossamer cat's-cradle, spun out of my inner being, was so fine that the slightest breeze disturbed it. My father's breath would have changed its colour and texture and left a coated veneer on the coruscating lace. My thoughts were trapped in that web; they shone as images.

Part of me was resigned to staying and part to breaking out in a display of outrage. The dormant nerve sleeping in our feudal society was susceptible to being awakened. Something in that dead synapsis wanted to flicker alive and orientate towards the challengingly antagonistic. A clown's mask suddenly appearing in the middle of a crowd of uniform, grey faces. Dione pushed things to the edge. He appeared out of nowhere at the blue end of an afternoon in red satin trousers and a black blouson. His walk suggested the supreme arrogance of the untouchable, the creature who appeared to owe nothing to his species but a contemptuous disdain. Hands jutting on his hips, mouth delineated by a red pencil, Dione was the androgynous manifestation who both fascinated and repelled.

I listened to the wind flick a fine spray against the window. The night was pushing its blue-black fur around the house. Something was rising within me, impelling me to break out and head for the shelter of the Beach Café where our group met each night. The café was a wooden shack painted white, with blue window-frames. It squatted on the sill of the beach and resembled a ship waiting to refloat on the incoming tide. At night it was the refuge of a secret society, a fraternity who came here secure in the knowledge they would be accepted. There was a juke-box loaded with warped 45s that boasted records by Edith Piaf, Barbara, David Bowie, Lou Reed, whoever made life into the taste of a bitter blue rose petal and then lifted a torch to celebrate the moment of one's being triumphantly alive and at odds with a conformist society. There was the voice of Dusty Springfield reaching the innermost chord of loneliness, evoking the solitary one who gets up from a crowded room and goes out on to a white veranda and stares off into a landscape empty as a photograph by Edward Weston.

This late-night spot attracted people from the waterfront. Tourists, boys and girls made up for all-night parties, the solitary who sat drinking and staring out to sea where a lighthouse punctually beat out a coded rhythm, and those who like ourselves came here to be accepted. One could sit and be, or pick up in a wall mirror the reflection of scarlet hennaed hair and a mouth crayoned the dark maroon of the single carnation placed in a tall-stemmed glass on each table. Men sat here as though they were huddled at the end of the world, in a whitewashed shack confronting the void, the black waters of the future. The place was like a beacon in the night to the lonely. They sat there, resolute, hunched into themselves, only reluctantly conceding to go home when a green streak in the sky predicted a false dawn. I used to wonder if these men worked, and if by day they erased the make-up from their faces and lived up to the conformist expectations of an insular community. Or did they – outsiders whose private incomes or approach to life allowed them an unrestricted liberty – go back to apartments and sleep until noon? They fascinated by their mythic adoption of the night journey. I might have expected to see them assemble under the red light at the end of the stone jetty and embark on a black death-ship steered by an old man in a boating cloak.

I decided to risk the consequences and escape there for the night. No one came to my room in the evenings. It was presumed that my guilt would be paid for in terms of study. And this time the pull in me was stronger for the knowledge that the girl who had so briefly approached me on my entrance to the gardens would be there. During these days of intense contemplation her face had come back to me, her eyes the green of peridots, her oval-shaped face inviting that I inquire of its sensitivity. And the more I attempted to form a synthesis of my fragmented memories of the Beach Café, the more her face imposed, so that I could recollect her being there on nights I had forgotten, a shadow figure watching me in a room full of smoke. Now I could see her more clearly. She had sat at a table between a blond acquaintance of Dione's and a girl-friend with a hooped gold earring that extended beyond the rim of her cheek. I had felt someone watching me, her eyes touching me lightly as moths, her breath arriving as a shadow that sensitized me into an involuntary awareness that I was being watched. I must have dismissed the possibility that such a girl would wish to speak to me, but at the same time the impression made on me had registered like a coloured thread of ink in water that months later was still insoluble. A green strand that had remained to become two eyes – underwater irises – openings into the inner world of a stranger. And there were other times when I must have been watched, and the little impressions that are so meaningful to another manifested themselves in characteristics of which I was unaware. It was this that intrigued me: the idea that we attract another without our ever knowing it. We orchestrate an ambience that lives as a defining quality, and this black-haired girl had picked up on the something that was me.

    I got out by way of a window that gave on to a grass track which lay parallel to the house. Already I could hear the sea, and the distant crash of breakers precipitated my wired-up flight. A prickling rain was carried by the wind and a brown moon was intermittently visible between flying cloud.

    In ten minutes I would be at the café. I could hear the matrix of the shore's pebbles grating with the turbulent groundswell. The beach was being turned on a lathe. The summer had broken with this storm sea; I thought of it as a turquoise vase smashed into wind-scattered fragments. The long, seamless months that had seemed pitched like a gold tent on the horizon were flawed by the big seas. I walked into the brunt of the wind; blue-black breakers were threatening to rise over the sea-wall. Ahead of me the café looked as if it were being dragged out to sea. White on white it was in contention with the high surf. The lights were on against a black backdrop.

For a long time I stood outside, delaying my entry. The wind was trapped inside my shirt like a bird struggling to get free. I was on the brink of a discovery, a realization that had already been decided within me. This one face had brought me here in the night through the interaction of an unresolved psychic need. A confused medley of voices and music opened up intermittently on the wind. When I pushed the door to it was like walking into a frieze inside my head – the lights, the faces were as I had imagined them – so that it seemed a deception, a trick of time, as though the scene was the same one and Nicholas still alive, seated at a table in the far corner of the room, discussing a novel or the metaphysical conundrum of the future.

Two or three faces that I recognized from the beach looked up at me with the suppressed sympathy of those who assume they are initiates to a secret that binds by a conspiratorial silence. The two egg-headed men, their ovoid-shaped skulls sun-bronzed and polished, were occupying their usual table with a youth whose blond hair spilled on to an orange jumper. All three of them were smoking black cigarettes. The two older men may have been lovers, brothers, twins, their corresponding white knitted ties and black shirts copied to the last studied affectation, that of leaving the bottom of their two cuff-fastening buttons open to reveal the hint of a gold bracelet.

I got to an empty table lit up by the green flash of the juke-box, not daring to look around to see if the girl was there.

Rather I took it as incontrovertible that she would be. I huddled into myself and began filling the blank snow-screen of a page with words. As long as the black ink-marks showed up I was safe – they represented the mental imprints that saved me from the void. I had abandoned song lyrics and Rubella's unreliable stage history for a deepening awareness of poetry. I wanted to find a lyric that would encapsulate not only our summer but also my psychological interpretation of those I had known, the faces gathered here, the inconstancy of human relations.

I remained fixed by the magic dance of words, the coruscating interplay of images that could establish an independent world, a house built out of crystal blocks into which I could peer again and again as into a rock-pool. I who had created this construct from the inside was now exiled into the role of an observer. I couldn't get back inside; the reflective surface of words prevented it.

As I puzzled over my creation I had the impression I was being watched. Perversity had me keep low, my head targeted above the page, my interest confined to myself. I was the luminous core of a star without radials. People were trying to attract my attention: I could feel the invidious intrusion of the blond boy with his two older companions trying to catch my eye. An eye-beam was jabbing at my glass and then playing across the more vulnerable areas of my face and eyes.

I continued to contract. I had practised this technique to a fine art – I could eliminate everything extraneous to my inner focus and render myself invulnerable. To reach me from the outside would be like forcing a window that gave on to a diamond interior.

Very cautiously my eyes rather than my head completed the fractions of a semicircle. My vision took in the blur of a table-lamp and the cuff of a green jumper. I knew it was hers, a green that would match her eyes, pick out the tidal waters surrounding the pupil's black abyssal O, and so concentrate one's emotions into that ambience. I resumed placing exaggerated emphasis on my cup of coffee. My mind was hallucinating images as I burnt up in a crucible of indecision. How could I ever forget the faces that rose before me like an elegy? The thrill of kissing a young man in lipstick, the pink bee-sting it imparted to the nerves, there under the shadow of the sea-wall in the high noon, just a few paces away from the unsuspecting. We were set apart by the daring that our instincts excited. I had come in that time to adopt a whole code of life that belonged to a minority. Things happened in our world through unexpected contacts – the spontaneity of a summer picnic in the hills, blue wine by a blue stream, after the day had started with the expectation of nothing more than the intention to visit the beach. There would be invitations to ski in Chamonix, visit the grape harvest in Aquitaine, suddenly one would find oneself drawn into a roof-garden party in a house one had often admired in passing but never dreamt of entering. The pink-haired owner, who boasted a residence in every Southern country, was here only three weeks a year. But the interior was suddenly open and made available to us because we were young and different. Doors opened at any time; the fraternity's resources for surprise and wealth were endless. I sat there battling with everything I had known. To renounce all this for the conventional seemed an impossibility. The bottles of perfume I kept hidden in my clothes drawer, the little black suede cosmetic bag with its eye pencils, foundation, lipsticks, all of these things had come to comprise a way of life. What I imagined without them was a life as conformist as my father's and the millions of men who seemed to inhabit only a part of themselves. They lived without sensitizing the feminine within them, and so denied themselves the chance ever to understand women. They constituted a nucleus that was impervious to fission. Unsensuous, masculine, dominated by preconceptions of gender, they were represented by our fathers and those before them.

My whole life swung in the balance of turning round, and by degrees I did so, finding her eyes meeting mine with the same smile as they had once come at me near the sea. Only this time it was more expressive of an emotion shared, an understanding of a process that had deepened by mutual reflection.

And having turned, I was in effect found out. There could be no revocation of the act unless I was to get up now and exit dramatically into the night.

When I looked up again she had joined me. There was her shadow on the wall and her face opposite. She was smiling at me without looking. It was as though my face were drawn in the table-top. I might have been lying there with her kneeling above, looking down. She was feeling a way forward, slowing her thoughts until they arrived at the right point of departure. Words would have broken the spell, but they would have to come, their indices played out like a series of white arrows on a black road.

'I've been thinking of you.' She smiled. 'That time at the garden, I didn't really know what to say. It must have seemed odd, my appearing like that without warning.' And as she spoke I was reliving it; the bay the blue of cineraria; the horizon drawn taut. At that moment I hadn't considered the possibility of an alternative life, I was shut into the one existence, the garden with its stone lions and urns, its scarlet geraniums, its beds of pink and violet petunias. I had known one way in a small world.

'And I've been thinking of you,' I said, conscious as I spoke of how I had buried her face and reclaimed it. It had been lying in the green depths of my mind waiting to be retrieved and lifted from the water like a shell.

'I've been watching you for a long time,' she resumed. 'I used to see you going to the beach each day, only I couldn't follow you. I've learnt a lot about you from a distance.'

I was conscious of the world contracting to this table with

its one pink, one red carnation. It was like a lunar beach, an emptiness across which two figures faced each other, both too confused to know why they had drifted out there through a cosmic flaw.

Diana's lips were a dark satin bow. She had the pencilled eyebrows of a Kiki de Montparnasse and green lozenge earrings that showed beneath her short, layered black hair. Her eyelids were powdered green and lilac. I could hear the hum of her being, the inner chord that vibrated with the interplay of her emotions and speech. I could sense the quiet within her, the enlivened impulse that generated excitement, the return swing of the balance to her still centre. There was no need for speech. Somehow we already knew each other well enough to dispense with words.

I could hear Rubella drunk at a table in the other corner of the room. The place was designed to resemble a ship's cabin. There were wheels and an anchor on the wall and, in keeping with the spirit, a number of French sailor's hats, blue with red pompons, were hung up above photographs of Dietrich and the flouncily coquettish Louise Brooks. I hoped Dione wasn't with Rubella's company. In an exaggeratedly camp voice she was calling for champagne and a silk slipper. I had seen out of the corner of my eye, by a process of fractional oblique perception, that she was with two of Dione's acquaintances, a home help to a company director and a seasonal employee in one of the waterside hotels. Exhibitionistic, drunk, falsetto, their voices were beginning to shrill. In my mind I was expecting Dione's sudden, dramatic entry, a feather boa wreathed around a sequined evening jacket, his taxi going back along the coast road to return at an appointed hour in order to take him and his friends to a last night-spot before home.

I was impatient to go, despite the presence of a fraternity by which I was accepted. I wanted the sea-wind to make me conscious of the nerve-spots that responded to the cold. After months of unrelieved torridity one had forgotten the extremes of contrast. The sea had grown to an agitated black and green pampas. I knew that the squint-eyed lighthouse would be twitchy with its regulated flash. Even if the coast had claimed Nicholas, its seas were in my blood. That measured wall of surf tilting at the shore in its staggered infolding rush was the high point of universal momentum. An end and a beginning – the wave expended, backtracking from swash into the hammock of the incoming, glaucous wave ribbed with diagonals of light.

I was hoping we could leave inconspicuously. There wasn't anywhere to go except out into the night. But somehow that didn't matter. What was important was the sympathetic link we had established without words, the sense of sharing the moment without having to qualify the experience by language. Words had come to represent building blocks which the sea knocked down unless they were given the substance of life on a page.

'I'll follow you out,' the girl said, sensing my disquiet, my mental impulse to be gone in the direction of my thoughts. When I slipped outside, the rain had stopped. The night air stood on my skin like grass. The sea was a white bear rolling on its back in the hollow. Instinct had me walk towards the place I knew so well. I was polarized to that ivied recess, the spotlights sunk in the flower-beds, the furtive shadows of men chalked up against stone. Someone had been knifed there one night, his name written up in blood on the shelter wall.

There wasn't any other direction to my life, just this narrow path winding above the sea. The barely audible footsteps behind me found my own and quite suddenly there were two of us acquiring no more space than one. I wasn't even anticipating a word, a gesture; the understanding was complete.

We stopped short of the entrance to the garden. There were figures above us, their movements amplified by the surrounding night. They were the ones Dione called panthers – the night visitors to this place who wished to remain anonymous outside of a small clandestine circle. They were there for casual sex or pick-ups in their cars.

We kept out of the promenade lights, mauve and green Chinese lanterns which were strung up each summer to form a necklace around the coast. We passed under the garden wall, the bank of pink lilies looking like huddled, sleeping flamingos in the subdued lighting. Just round the bend of the cove in which we swam was a shelter that looked out over the marina and the cobalt waters of the night bay.

It was like moon-walking, the unreality of my being here, walking side by side with someone I knew by intuitive sympathy – and trusted implicitly. We sat down, smelling the tonic salt in the air, the iodine tang of kelp glistening like a chestnut mare in rain, all along the high-water mark. Suddenly there was nothing to fear. I had become conditioned to the reflexional panic that a stranger's presence incited. So many men stepped out of the noon or dark and all of them were in search of the elusive stranger they were unable to find. Their need to impose a shield against loneliness was so great that they would accept the most absurd compromise. In this way they were in turn deluded, deceived, robbed and beaten. Max, with a blue billiard pocket beneath his left eye, explaining it away to his colleagues, a blond boy somewhere loose with his wallet, emptying cash on clothes and finally crawling back to plead for shelter.

I had to convince myself that this was happening. It hardly seemed possible that I was on the threshold of a new sexual awakening. The images of my past were slowing down, they were no longer a herd of threatening black stallions surrounding a lonely farm. I could see Diana's red bra-strap where it had slipped wide of her sweater, ridged into her bronze skin. We sat side by side opposite the white, searching eye of an offshore lighthouse. I had only to move my denimed leg to be in contact with hers.

As I sat back from her it occurred to me that she was the opposite to what I had known and yet the same. Her make-up, her clothes, the green lakes sunk in her eyes, the quiet movements of her body, all of this could have been the deception to which I was accustomed. I was curious to know how her mouth would fit mine, how her fingers would ignite my nerve-points. And how far would she want me to go if I once began. I could feel a dull, insistent throbbing in my cock. I wasn't frightened of rejection; I had only to turn her towards me to discover the intensity of her passion. He-shes and She-hes had been the normative rule of my life. My mother and father stood outside as oddities. They had still to encounter the change I saw waiting for them on the other side of the glass. There were angels who would instruct them at the edge of the world, and androgynize their unilateralism.

My pulse was beginning to race. What happened was so sudden it was like piercing a raspberry on one's nether lip and feeling the juice activate the palate. It was the taste of surprise that flooded me as my lips found hers and followed their circular motion. Correspondingly my hands came up inside her jumper and moulded themselves to her breasts. Her body resonated; it was sinuously alive.

My tongue worked to extract a source which eluded me. We resembled two people desperately seeking a knowledge which is implanted in the other. We feared to disengage in case we drew apart to find no one there, only the imaginary face that was now swimming against one's own in the union of two masks. And there was only the deepening response, the fury at being unable to penetrate the barriers imposed by flesh. Her fingers found the nerve-points in my waist and spine. They went on exploring, feeling the furnace grow in me. Our mouths were seeking an impossible dialectic. The sea was part of this; breakers ran at a half-tilt before expending themselves in a white torrent over the opposing shingle gradient. Their roar answered the greater build-up in our

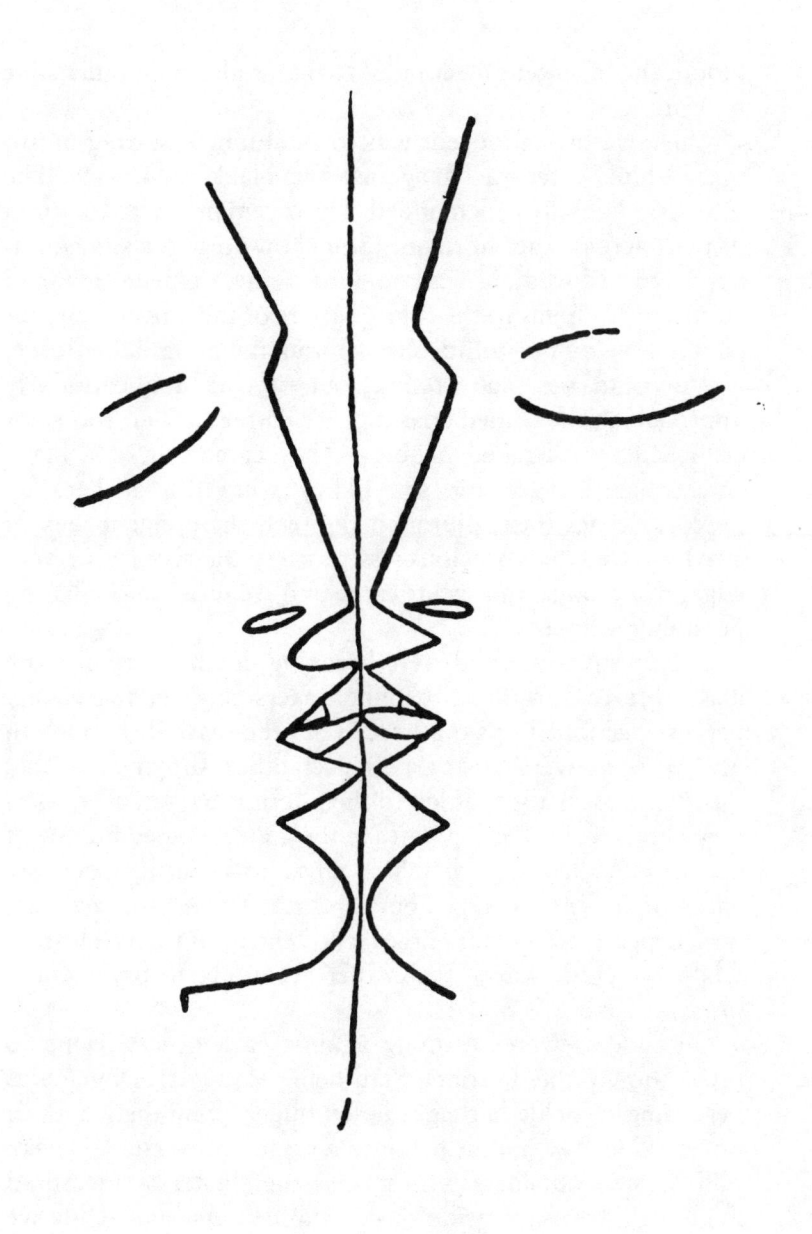

blood, the insurgent meeting of two seas above an indivisible barrier.

When we broke loose it was to sit stunned, staring out to sea. White water raced against the black night sky. The dramatic backdrop demanded a proscenium, a red curtain drawn across the horizon. Somehow the sea's vastness appeared reduced; it was no longer the element that had stretched Nicholas to the four quarters of the universe. It was containable by our jointly confronting its indomitable force.

We could see men coming out of cars and cautiously approaching the ruined coastguard's cottage. Their footsteps crunched over packed pebbles. They came out of a black velvet bag hungry for sex. They were drawn here by inexorable ties, fast, plural encounters, the pungent reek of amyl nitrate, the voraciousness to carry the risk to the very edge. They came and went, came and went on an oscillating pendulum of need.

The misgivings I had were breaking down. I began more and more to surrender to light fingers that set fire to my nerves, cushioned tips that traced out the sensual channels in my body. We were closing in on each other, slipping invisibly through glass walls that led to the interior. My own exploratory hands were creating notes in the guitar-shaped hollow of her back. A silent wind had blown us into a roaring forest fire whose flames never singed but caressed. The pressurized heat was dependent on our striking a centre, a forest clearing where we could know each other according to psychic and physical dictates.

Our bodies were straining against each other, trying to break down the barriers that kept us apart. Diana was beginning to tickle her right index finger along the length of my erection. We had drawn into a crystal universe. We were oblivious to outsiders who passed the shelter at measured intervals. We were inside the crystal's facets, and while we could look out at the night, others would be blinded by our refraction. I was straining to release myself from the constriction of tight denims – jeans that were styled according to sailor's pants and had a line of visible red buttons rather than a zip-fastener for a fly. Diana's fingers found these out one by one, lingering slowly over each, deliberately restraining from accelerating the process as a lacquered fingernail made contact with my flesh. A second and a third finger began to strike up a frictional movement. When I felt her lips go down on me the pressure had become a volcano-head.

As I started to come, the lava drawn out through a constrictive eye, I was aware once more of journeying through a forest to find a face I had always known but never realized hidden in deep foliage. It might have been my double: the holistic feminine within me externalized without the conflicting male properties.

We walked back to the accompaniment of a silent music. The surf was throwing up high over the stone jetty and seawall. Red lights shone inside the café like marker beacons. We neither of us even asked for the other's address, for we would find each other anywhere and always. I knew that a letter would come for me within days, confirming all that I had felt most deeply.

We parted at the café, I to return home to the sleeping house and she to walk entranced, somewhere, and finally to stop at a house I had already imagined as hers. One that looked out to sea, its windows open on the stars.

Chapter 6

Rain blurred the prospect. It drew a taut line of verticals across the windows. I lay with an ear to the radio and an eye on the page. The house was empty, for I had established my own inner kingdom; I had withdrawn so deep into myself that I was inaccessible to my parents. There were five days to go before we entered our last year of education or broke loose to follow the scene on its dizzy, hedonistic course through parties to spiralling social intrigue.

Poetry had become the crystal city through which I walked at night. Its luminous houses, built out of symmetrically proportioned facets, contained images of such blinding intensity that I sat transfixed, staring at the prismatic quality of visual symbols. There was no way in to the geometrically refractive city; I had to sit outside and be patient.

Nicholas's death was slowly becoming a reality. He no longer floated suspended but had sunk to a level that was out of reach during the day, submersively opaque, and only at night did he acquire the outline of something phosphorescent – the drowned man rolling over in the current, mouth twisted open as though forced by fingers.

I had deliberately not seen Diana since that first night. There was more pleasure in the perversity of waiting. It was my distraction with the inner world that prevented me from going back to the Beach Café and finding her. Each night I planned a return and retracted at the last moment. I preferred to imagine our meeting rather than experience it. The excitement was building in me night after night towards some dramatic dénouement.

When a letter came it was from Dione. It was left on the window-sill of my room after a perfunctory tap on the glass, so as to elude my parents' detection. The note was on a page of deckled pink paper folded inside a grey envelope. The message was brief and forbidding.

There's a meeting at the garden at 4.30 tomorrow. For your own sake I advise you to attend. It's paramount. Mother's in the chair.

Dione

There was no time for equivocation. I imagined Dione officiating over a black court, his ruthlessly cutting indictments turned upon the nerves like broken glass.

I lay back and luxuriated in the moment. Between now and then stretched an indefinite curve which consciousness could protract by its immediacy of awareness. The graph took in poems, Diana, Rimbaud's *Une saison en enfer,* which I was reading, and the night which was still to come, when once again I would rehearse slipping out to the Beach Café, only to remain chin against the window, listening to surf level its white thunder across the shore.

And the future? Always that improbable void. We had lived through so much already on an inner plane that to advance was to confront a furnace. 'Autumn already....' Tonight I would go out and risk everything, thereby weakening the hold that Dione had over Paul, Rubella and me. I would burn inside the dark: I would strike a light against a cliff-face and watch the faces shine out in their petrified malevolence. Poetry was a key to this blazing. If a poem worked the fire within, it was constant.

Regardless of my parents' restrictions I decided to go out as soon as it was dark. The rain had let up; pink, zeppelin-shaped clouds nosed into a dark-blue whirlpool. My preparations were a fetishistic ritual. I inhaled the musky scent of my leather jacket and slipped on a red silk neckscarf to offset a matelot's striped vest and blue denims. My nerves craved for the kicks that Dione so relished – the spiral into an illusory fourth dimension, sex magnified by plurality, the drug releasing its delayed star-flash.

I got out under the early dark, a peppermint-green rift of sky showing above the sea. Lights had come on in the high-rises around the coast; thousands of orange rectangles set in the dark. It was the hour when the singer was conveyed across a city cushioned in the back of a silver-white limousine, a blonde, leather-skirted girl holding his champagne glass. The hour when the poet walks out in search of the unnamed mystery – the white rainbow that intersects with the perfect curve of space.

After a night of storm the bay was calm. The undertow was turbulent with groundswell, but a green-black glassy surface caught the reflection of the coloured lanterns. I decided to stop at the Beach Café before going on. There was still the possibility of something happening that would alter my life, the epiphanic moment consuming me in the ash of change.

One could tell it was the end of the season. The hotel lounges overlooking the bay seated a third of their capacity. Waiters attended the tables with more accented assiduousness. In another month they would make the return trip to Lisbon or Madeira.

The equinox had left a white head on the water; it had changed the sea from a crystalline blue to a transpicuous grape-green in the shallows. The surf was making frisky strides inshore. In two hours it would be climbing the sea-wall, licking the overhang with its foment.

I had nothing to lose. I entered the café, not as one weighed down by a psychological complicity in Nicholas's death, but as someone desperate to reverse the march of time and live so intensely in the here and now that tomorrow would be a prolongation of that heightened sensory experience. There were groups of men gathered at tables, some of whom I recognized from the beach, while others were newcomers, tourists come to realize the last mellow light of a late amber sun. I took a table close to the juke-box. I primed the records to fall in accordance with my mood. Bowie's 'Watch That Man' zipped into an accelerative upbeat mood – 'a lemon in a bag/did the tiger rag' – and my mind went out on a corresponding trajectory. It was Dione who said we should live like the stars, Dom Perignon for breakfast, Chanel No. 5 fragranced into our underwear, night rides under the stars, the chauffeur wearing lipstick and a black face-net, the car cruising at ninety all the way along the fog-bushed blue highways of L.A.

After Bowie the music changed to Iggy Pop's 'Lust for Life', and the voltage thugging through my nerves as the powerful opening lines drove out every other consideration but the urgency of the message.

>Here comes Johnn Yen again
>With his liquor and drugs
>With his liquor and drugs
>He's gonna do a striptease.
>Hey man you got that lotion
>With your torture machine. . . .

I could feel the decibel count communicating with my nervous electricity – I wanted to reach a state of irreversible euphoria, a propulsion that would drive me unthinkingly into the eye of the furnace. I was beginning to catch fire and lose consciousness of my immediate surroundings. I was living out an anticipated fantasy . . . running through a forest towards a red and gold floral perianth, sunflowers whipped my shoulders, androgynous creatures dropped down to the earth from blue foliage. There would be a summation to this in the hills, out of sight and out of ear. . . .

When the third record dropped on to the turntable it was Lou Reed's 'Waiting for the Man' – the tempestuous live version that moved with defiant, accelerative speed towards a shattering climax.

> Feel sick and dirty
> More dead than alive
> I'm waiting for the man
> I'm waiting for the man. . . .

We had spent our lives waiting for the man and always the wrong one. He was a mask behind a mask behind a mask. If he stepped clear of his disguise he wouldn't know himself any more than we would him. He was the inaccessibly elusive, the one who was never there or present when we didn't recognize him. His properties were those of never owning to human ties; the hand he offered froze on contact; the promises he made floated out to sea like red balloons on a fête day. When you reached his address, he hadn't been heard of for three years. His office hadn't ever employed anyone of that name; the man didn't feature in the directory. When you finally got a number it was his wife who answered, saying they had divorced three years ago and to the best of her knowledge her husband was dead.

I followed my own drift of thought to its series of indistinct conclusions. The possibilities that presented themselves seemed to confirm the condition of hopelessness that had so quickly descended. The only way out was through inner space. The chances of a fiction materializing in which I would be spirited away to Paris, Zurich or New York, seemed increasingly remote. My expectations were starting to plummet; my actual acquaintances compared with my imagined ones seemed depotentialized, impotent to effect radical changes.

I sat waiting for my elusive chance. Tomorrow it would be too late; Dione would have resumed his superiority and the summer disappeared like a migrant bird into the blue, Southern spaces. I imagined sails burning in a harbour, a mad sailor walking the quay playing an accordion, lost fleets nosing in from the sea-roads. A man was attempting to have me follow his eye, but I knew better. I went deeper inwards where he couldn't reach. I was looking for the beautiful one, the elusive face whose only command is that we follow, no matter the time of the day or the place, for the moment will never come again. The lines that gave birth to this stranger were effortless. I followed my green-eyed vision across the page.

The Beautiful One

Again, and with amazing clarity
was there to see, a street scene, blond in fog,
or red-haired on a russet autumn day,
seen disappearing behind a beech tree
into a smoky wood, the leaf-twinkle
brighter for that – the memory
adumbrated by a black cape, then lost
to cloudings, disillusionments, unreal
stabs made at identity, curious
speculations concerning he or she,
and always different, improbably beautiful,
but brief, like a sea elegy,

a fragment in the Greek anthology
for a drowned sailor run into a squall.
And there were other vestiges as brief,
the precision in ducking from a car
into a sealed lobby, and once in dark glasses
holding a green drink in a bar,
then disappearing through the mazes of Montmartre,
already a legend, the golden one
who never ages – for his fictional
existence is outside of time, his face
adaptable to any shift of plane.

We lived for his inventiveness, wrote scripts
to be handed to intermediaries
and waited, patient where malachite stairs
dropped to a river, for his coming there,
collar turned up, a red glow in the mist
catching our cold, breath-stencilled memories.

 I should like to have begun living where the poem ceased. Each image demanded I pursue its transient beauty through an inner landscape coppered by autumn. A rose-pink mist laid wreaths over Montmartre, and later the unexpected stairs, the drop to the river where before had been a wall enclosing a ruined orchard. I wanted life to be like this: the marvellous transposed into a cinematic sequence. One would follow blue roads out of the town at nightfall and discover a château hidden behind dense woods. There would be a man sitting at a desk writing, a naked woman sitting on his lap, her blonde hair establishing curtains over the page. When he breathed into her hair, it raged like a forest fire but the page remained uncharred.
 I was hardly conscious that someone else had entered the café through the sea-facing glass door. I was still chasing the poem's afterglow, its red singeing mist, the oars dipping the water like a swan's lifted wings.

When I looked up, she was sitting opposite me – Diana with her green eyes and perfectly shaped red lips. She had given emphasis to her lipstick bow by delineating it with a dark pencil. Her eyelids were powdered gold and green and red. Her hand found mine on the table-top effortlessly. She didn't say anything; her eyes expressed a level of consciousness that was already compensating for my awkward silence. She was here again, this girl who had stood between me and the night. The light in her face must have reached me, for I looked up and smiled as a slow saxophone wailed from the juke-box. It was like meeting in a film, this silent encounter of eyes as a jazz record evoked blue April skies coming clear after rain, a young man running out of breath in pursuit of a girl beneath bridges of the Seine, who turns round in a violet dress to catch his hand and dance beside the water, she throwing his gift of roses one by one into the swirling current.

I had somehow gone beyond the poem into life, as though the lateral points of the one had extended into the other. Diana had become the poem's exteriorization, the one who most closely identified with its psychic field. The vibration set up by images had drawn her to find a reflection in the poem's crystal.

She was wearing a black jumper with rhinestones sewn on the shoulders and a short, black, woollen skirt. I noticed the difference in her face, how her hair being parted on the left and swept to the right accentuated her forehead, the green pencilled eyebrows being given greater prominence in defining her locket-shaped face. She expressed no disquiet at not having heard from me, but affirmed the moment, the intensity of here and now, the tension field of just being before that expression is put into words. Diana accepted it as natural that we should both be here in a café notorious for its sexual assignations. She seemed to be acquainted with most of the clientele, and so my fears of having to explain the past were allayed. Nights in the moving circle of a black necklace, serpents tattooed on arms, and the trust needed to make a stranger come out of the dark. Diana was none of these things, and yet she had lived through it all by a kind of empathy.

Her right hand interlaced with my left. We were moving towards a deeper union, something exploratory and sure in its still unconceived design, but already there by anticipation. I had planned the night to be one of wildfire adventure, but this hand, these lips, constituted a magnetism.

The last orange and green sunset embers had conceded to indigo. The points that I knew so well along the coast were lighting up. It was both a celebration and an elegy, this living out of the irrevocable passage of time. My youth was buried on the beach like a sand-castle flooded by the tide.

The café was beginning to fill up. A party of young men accompanied by a girl in a tight, red, sequined skirt sat at the table opposite. They looked to be of predominantly ambivalent gender – eyes that would take on either sex. They would move on by degrees to night-spots, clubbing until the dawn found them with transient partners.

The whole summer was running at me like a surf-wall. Dione had spoken of it as a threshold, a trampoline leap into a dizzying succession of penthouse gardens. One would be greeted there by women with the visual beauty of Man Ray's La Marquise Casati, with her black lips, white face and raindrop eyes, giving the impression of being doubled, the lower like a mask beneath a black silk fringe. But somewhere a gap had established itself. I needed words as the connection between the two states: departure and arrival.

We left the café and went down and stood on the beach facing the advancing tide. Breakers crashed over the pebble-line and advanced in white jags up the beach. There was nothing between us and the horizon but the purple night sea. Everything and nothing could happen; youth burning out in the roar of blood and surf as our bodies meshed, delirious, frantic to erase consciousness of anything but the instant.

Chapter 7

In my dream there was a black snake poking its head out of the trumpet of an arum lily. I awoke and turned over on the picture of Dione's face which eluded focus. It spun away from me like the spiral of a bright coin falling through water. When I next caught up with it, he was playing a small hand-drum at the bottom of a steep cliff. When he turned round to face me he was wearing a white mask with a thin stream of blood escaping from the mouth. The scene changed to one of flight. I chased him through moonlit alleys to a stone house marked with a black cross. When I went in through a door, the interior was dark. There was no one there. A green lamp was lit on a black table-top. There was a fox's head mounted on the wall and two bloody tears rolled out of its eyes, red tadpoles that converged on the pointed snout. Suddenly it was Dione who, by an abrupt transition, was staring out of the animal's eyes. The mouth opened and shrieked – nothing else, just this savage, ululating scream, a vixen's challenging assertion to a male picking up scents at the edge of a twilit wood.

I was catapulted out of the house into a street scene. A war or natural catastrophe must have occurred, for the place was devastated. The buildings were lying down horizontally: an orange bulldozer was swinging at a wall on which a tiny figure stood waving his arms. Each time the bulldozer flattened a section of the wall, the part still intact increased proportionately in height. I tried to follow this telescoping into the sky. There weren't any clues as to who I or the other was. The latter's voice couldn't be heard. He was waving a black scarf at me, a banner proclaiming liberty or death. When the next sequential flash occurred, there were guards on the wall. A huge red bloodstar was pulsating on the concrete. The figure which had initially attracted my attention was laughing. He was performing a cabaret song, with a black hat, black leather shorts, a silver-ferruled cane.

I forced myself out of the dream. It was like breaking through a series of glass walls that were transpicuous as air. I shot upwards through black to blue to clear to air. The day was on the other side, an orange sunlight meeting my bed as my mind fixed into the nagging reality of having to meet Dione later in the day. He would hold melodramatic court over our depleted and disbanding group. The first yellow leaves would drift out on the sea as a token that the heat-wave had come to an end. Thereafter we would be transformed, stripped like the leaves on the mulberry, pressed into stark relief as shadows inhabiting a stone wall in winter sunlight.

My clothes from the previous night lay discarded at random on the bed. They were dusted with sand. An unconscious sense of disfigurement recalled me to the love-bites which Diana had strung together across the base of my neck and above each hip. These surface contusions shone like magenta marbles suffused with blue. Fatigue had left me dissociated from my body. I had shared myself with her on that night beach; we had lain like the outgoing wave in the arms of its forward-rolling successor. I felt enervated but psychically fulfilled. I kept feeling for the trapdoor that would open into a false bottom, but it didn't come. Diana had imparted sufficient of herself to allow me to feel buoyed up, sustained against whatever recriminations would come in the course of the day.

The day was amber shot with the promise of warmth by noon. It was always like that at the end of the summer vacation. One was led to believe in an illusory suspension of the fall, days in which the air stood still and someone seemed always to be calling one's name from the other side of the bay.

This time I had Diana's address. She had written it on the page opposite my last poem. The two sychronized as I recalled the night, the heavy pounding of surf drumming the beach on which we had made love. I recalled the scene with luminous, oneiric consciousness. Our bodies were like bright fish jumped out of the wave to thrash on the sand.

I knew I would spend the day occluded by the prospect of meeting Dione. I sensed that the afternoon would mark a definitive break with youth ... I wanted to get out of the house early and prepare myself by waiting in the shelter above the sea. Everything that had marked the precipitant rush of our lives to date, our lack of time in which to acquire a critical perspective, the intensity with which we had lived through things that would take on their real significance only much later, was about to be extinguished.

Paul had anticipated my own intention to arrive early. I found him sitting on a bench screened by pink hydrangeas, the morose positioning of his hands, the concentration expressed in his face telling me that he too was reliving a journey through the past, a realization of a passage come this far to end on a white beach. He was dressed casually in a black jacket and blue jeans with a white, open-collar shirt. He looked up as though expecting me. It was easy like that with him, his simplicity dispensed with formalities. He was anxious. The strain imposed on his life by Nicholas's death and the duplicity of being here again as an outsider, a sexual outlaw, gave him the air of someone who weighed a hypothetical happiness against the psychophysical demands of his body. I noticed that he was wearing a thin gold bracelet for the first time; something to which he self-consciously returned, eyeing it with a fascination that denoted both reproach and a defiant vindication of his identity.

We listened to the slow dazzle of surf. We had known this place in so many different moods – fear, expectation, uncertainty, exalted euphoria – that we hadn't accounted for the final snap, the vertiginous realization that we were free now to negotiate life without its support. We couldn't imagine that: the world was an untried proposition, a universal sponge absorbing the anonymous, erasing its individual features. And we too were threatened with invisibility – cities, skyscrapers, the endless chain of faces observed under neon lights on a bridge, the descent into subways, the packed and jostled gasping for air in sealed interiors. Would we ever again recognize each other on emerging broken, drained by the day, to bloodless faces hanging out beneath viaducts, waiting for the big event that never came, the figure of a red satin heart spinning across the fields to the sunset?

I placed my hand lightly over Paul's and we stared at the indifferent horizon. Nothing in the out-there could intervene to help us. A glassy, aquamarine sea lifted its eye to the sky-face. Our only relationship with space was the glaze of air on our faces, our hands.

We talked of our restricted home-lives, the fears we entertained about the immediate future. Paul was rooted in his dilemma. If he got away, there could be no coming back. As an only son his flight would lead to his being disinherited. Father and son would meet in a dusty killing-field where a cow had once collapsed after miscarrying. Paul's father had shot it to prevent its bellowing, its blood seeping into the parched ground.

Everything we had lived through showed in our faces. The minatory play of night and day images, trooping out of the unconscious from earliest childhood to this moment in time, had in their alternation between light and dark shaped who we were, now in the moment of arresting flux. The continuity would always include these – oedipal myths, oneiric visions, the peopled world of inner space that went on independent of our involvement with the temporal. I kept on wondering what it would be like suddenly to enter Paul's stream of consciousness. Would it be a different world marked by colours and perceptions that were otherwise unknown to me, so that I found myself in a landscape without familiar landmarks, looking at things personalized by him and not me, individualized by stress notes marked on his reading of a place? It was what made human relations so poignant, this knowledge of the inaccessibility of another's mind. And once you became aware of that isolation, there was never again any help or way out of the lonely, rapid downstream movement towards death. It was as though our anxiety placed us apart, so that men entering the gardens paid us no attention, not even Max patrolling his hunting-ground on the way down to a deserted beach. We were alone. We had elected to undergo a trial which had no validity other than that it was deeply rooted in our respective psychologies. Rubella also, for all her unrestrained extroversion, her bodily magnetism, would come and face Dione's indictments. And there would be others too, the weak over whom he had asserted a blackmailing or drug hold, or perhaps a new lover whom he wished to humiliate and discard. His sneering, recriminatory manner was a corrosive acid. His smile could slash one's nerves.

There were oyster-catchers running the wave-line. We listened to their shrill outcry as their orange bills stabbed at an incoming wave. It was Paul who looked up and spoke: 'I've decided to go in a couple of months. I'd rather make a break ... things are too bad at home. Because of what's happened with Nicholas and the rumours about the place, my parents have decided to marry me to Suzanne. Arrangements are already going ahead. Can you imagine?'

His voice was weighted, undersea, not resigned but assertive of an additional reserve. Looking at his bracelet I wondered whether he had met someone with whom to take the leap across the gulf into the unknown. Paul had adopted the secrecy of a carp married to the depths of a murky pond. Nothing could make him rise above a certain level.

Neither of us could help the other. What came beyond this was a huge canvas that had still to be primed before we could splash it with hieroglyphic writing. I imagined our standing on opposite shores, one painting in red, the other in blue, and never once finding a shared image. We would go on doing this until our logograms were coloured vapour trails left on the sky.

I tried to disengage from the unreality of the situation. I knew that I had only to get up and walk down the sea-stairs and the impending crisis could be averted. But in a way it was already taking place. Dione had begun the process a long time ago and it was we who would conclude it with our own self-judgements. I could feel the fear of the abstract mounting; that half-heard shout from the opposite shore was returning.

I looked at Paul but he didn't seem to have heard it. There was only the audible rhythm of surf flicking a white crest out of the bay.

Who were they, the intruders into my mind? A headless horse charging through violet grasses, the ruined site of a temple overgrown with wild rose, a face with red lips that might have come out of Egon Schiele, the mosaic of images that moved like a cortège across the stream. It was so silent, this endless procession over which I seemed to assert so little power. Nebulae came and went, showed clearly or inarticulately before being swallowed by a black hole.

And what if they suddenly reversed order, the inner and outer worlds, so that I sat inside my head on a green bench overlooking a concave bay, staring out at a visually unedited inner dialogue?

Paul had closed up again. I might have left him and gone off to walk across the beach, only there was the same sense of an irrevocable magnetism. The scene had become an Aeschylean stage on which a roaring pyre would burn on the shore. A chorus would comment on our actions while a slow deathship entered the bay.

There was still time – it might have been minutes, years, centuries before Dione was due to show up. I wanted to go off alone and write a poem. Words would act as a brake on the inner whirl of images.

'I never told you', Paul said, 'how I first came across sex. I must have been eleven or twelve. There're a number of outhouses behind the farm. I used to go there to poke around amongst fertilizer sacks and rusty implements. Anyhow I went there one day to get out of the rain and heard what sounded like a struggle. Someone was breathing hard. I thought it must be one of the sheep or a calf taken ill. I hadn't heard that sort of breathing before. I went dead. I was too scared to move, and when my eyes got used to the dark I could make out a body struggling on top of another. I was terrified to move in case they heard me. When I got away and round the back I saw my father crouched down looking into the shed through the single low window. I ran. I just wanted to get away from what was happening and lose myself in the trees. After that there wasn't any going back to the way in which my father lived. . . .'

The pain was transposed to Paul's face. I could imagine the dusty, gold nimbus of light filtering into the darkened shed, and his father round the other side, flat on his knees, a voyeuristic eye adjusting and readjusting to the positional angles of the couple. And then Paul's long run across grey meadows into the vaulted interior of a wood.

And now Paul had spoken of it the incident hadn't diminished. On the contrary it had assumed other dimensions. The narrative had escaped, overreached its inner boundaries and become something that could be subjected to discourse. The mind as duality, as a two-way mirror. Paul would go on watching in my head, his confusion speaking of shock, excitement, the unreality enforcing itself as an incident in time, no matter how he closed his eyes or ran.

Paul looked at me in the hope that I might reciprocate his confession.

'It was different for me,' I said. 'I was forced out of curiosity to discover what I had expected. I used to follow couples into the long grass, drawn there by some need I couldn't name. I didn't really know what I would see or how to react in the event of it happening.'

'So you were like my father,' Paul said.

'It was more a compulsion. Then one afternoon I heard a woman's laugh. You know, that tinkling, excited laughter which is unmistakably sexual. It's something that hooks you more than any other sound. Once I'd located it, I closed in. The intermittent giggle caught in my throat. It remained trapped there like an explosive. In a way I didn't really want to see because hearing was seeing. What I saw was confused, blurry, hurried. A girl with floating blonde hair and dressed in a black slip was lying on top of a man who was dictating the rhythm of her body by rotating her bottom with his hands. . . .

'That was before I met a man who stepped out of the dark and kissed me. I had no sense of surprise. His gender didn't matter. What impressed me was his daring, his realization that I wouldn't resist his assertive advances. A woman wouldn't have dared to do that.

'I suppose that's why we're here. It's what Dione calls kicks. The search for unconventional sex.'

Paul looked away without speaking. The drift of our talk was like smoke rising from an autumn bonfire, bluish-grey whorls of memory biting at the olfactory senses. If a fog had risen now, obscuring the seascape, the opposite coast, it would have complemented our evocation of formative experience. Somewhere buried in the mica-schist of our past was the metamorphic chrysalis that had responded to an activating chemistry. An imbalanced chromosome, an overpronunciation of the anima, the buried woman in the psyche surfacing with ten candles between her fingers, her mouth a full-blown scarlet rose, her gold feet splayed on a lotus.

There was comfort in not knowing what we were. In that way we remained flexible – we were variant possibilities evading a norm. We could go with the stream, embrace a new species, jumping the gender barrier into the mutant pool of the twenty-first century.

The afternoon was being projected as a series of film stills. First, a blue bay. There's a single red sail inshore. Farther out, on a marbled white horizon brushed with lavender clouds, is a ship hanging on the skyline. Figure A shields his hands with his eyes and appears to be following the ship's progress. He appears to be observing the cedilla of smoke escaping from the ship's funnel.

Figures A and B are possibly being watched by a figure on the beach. The latter is still insufficiently defined, but clearer observation, which comes about owing to B's curiosity picking up on a motionless vertical slightly off-centre of his visual field, brings Figure X into play. She is a girl with dark hair dressed in a short, ruby-coloured blouson and tight black jeans. He decides to disregard her presence, making it incumbent on her to register an assocation by moving closer into the foreground.

It's possible that X can also observe Y, who is standing on a height above A and B, although to her he is as imprecise as she is to A if he has noticed her, and most certainly to B, who has already felt disquieted by her presence. Neither A nor B, who are both engaged in frontal vision, have observed Y, who seems to be looking through A and B to X. A tall cluster of raffish blue agapanthus is dwarfed by plumes of pampas-grass.

A and B have found a means of silent communion. A red admiral opens its wings in the sunlight like a scarlet and black pansy that has learnt how to fly. It has caught their attention, thus eliminating the growing pressure of X from B's immediate consciousness.

Y has begun slowly to move in on A and B, although each time he comes closer he arrests his progress and stands, chin resting on his right wrist, looking out to sea. His sleeve is of brilliant orange satin. His hair is hennaed red beneath a black beret.

Entering the picture, unobserved by X, A, B and Y, is a girl to be designated as R. She moves with the consciousness of someone truly involved in a film. She is aware of an inner choreography that provokes gestures. Dressed in a short gold-sequinned skirt, gold stilettos and a black silk top, her extravagant, ringleted hair shot through with the same gold as her skirt and shoes, she appears to dance more than walk. She has succeeded in creating around her the impassable distance which separates the stage from the audience. Her walk is a dance. The curvaceous rhythm of her body – one cannot imagine her immobile – sets up a resonance that engages the eye before the interplay of the other senses. R still hasn't seen Y, who may have grown aware of X, who appears to be cutting a line across the beach which will have her intersect with the steps directly beneath the bench occupied by A and B.

It is X who has become aware of Y, who has at this moment swung around to discover R, who kisses him on the lips. The action is complete in a stinging flash. What follows is a mutual excitement over clothes. R lifts up Y's puffed orange sleeve, and in doing so reveals a *diamanté* bracelet in the form of a serpent swallowing its tail.

They remain engaged in exclamatory discourse. Y facing R so that neither can have observed X disappear from the picture simultaneously with A and B, who appear to be intent on avoiding X's by now pronounced aim in joining them. X having increased her speed, has still to encounter a gradient of loosely packed granite and basalt pebbles which the tide has pushed to a slope on the immediate foreshore.

A and B have jointly disappeared around a circular bend in the gardens. They wade through a slope of tall grasses towards the derelict coastguard's house situated on the sill of the cove. They know that they are safe once they have acquired this refuge. X cannot be searching for both A and B. Her emotive field is directed towards B, who, suspended in mid-stride, can be seen to be dominating the flight, his right foot arching several paces clear of A, who is already slowing on the down-slope. Both are so involved in speed, in overtaking themselves, that A has broken into a laugh which has still to be seconded by B. They appear from this height to be running into the sea, for the sloping vertical that gives on to a narrow promenade drops steeply and inclines by a tuck in the overhang.

FLASH – and the sequence takes on its dramatic content.

'He's waiting for us,' Paul said. 'And that girl you know, Diana, she's somewhere around. Wasn't it her standing off on the beach?'

I could smell the impending crisis; it was sharp as the iodinic residue of kelp. The fragments of an imploded mosaic were coming together – irregular lapis lazuli pieces were magnetized into an integral dance. The hour struck with the impact of a blade. We were without warning suddenly facing Dione's accusing sneer. There were two youths placed to right and left of him whose purpose was unequivocally clear. One, with bleached peroxide hair and dressed in a short leather jacket, stood blocking the entrance to the building; the second, who was almost a facsimile of the first, was standing to the right of us, hands spread flat in his denim pockets, his apparent casualness confirming his minatory role.

Dione was wearing a flame-coloured orange blouse and black velvet trousers. He had pinned his hair beneath a black velvet beret. He was high on coke and sniffed periodically as though burnt by an irritant. His death was diagrammatically written beneath his features: it was there like an abstract geometry, a second self that would assume dominance when he accidentally overdosed.

I kept wondering what had brought us to this abandoned building, a rectangle of washed-out green sky making it through the wire netting of a window, while Dione partly blocked the light flooding the doorway. There was a smell of rust, damp, fungoid decay which not even the months of drought could eliminate. If the sky made it inside, it would solidify into a blue cube.

Paul stood hallucinated, looking right through Dione in a clear hole to the sea. He might have been frozen in the instant of watching an abrupt transition in a film. What was happening was so outside anything that his life could have prepared him for that I expected him to break apart in pieces.

Dione was fixing himself into his words, sniffing as though his senses were searching for a line.

'It wazz you two who killed Nicholas, thatz why you're hiding here.... We've come to sort you out. We want to know what happened.'

Each time he spoke it was as though he were falling through the air. His words went crashing into vertigo – they were like stones arriving out of space. His two clones smiled at whatever he said. Their co-ordinated responses failed to meet with the stress he placed on his words.

'Nicholass didn't drown. You guys killed him. We wazz watching. We saw you. Why don't you come straight?'

I could see Paul's body stiffen. His physical strength, his instinctive loathing of Dione's shambling, sibilant drawl, his trust, all of these things were affronted by the latter's arrogant sneer.

In the brief silence I could hear a plane go over, banking low above the bay. It added a dimension of space to our restricted movements.

Dione took a step inside the door, his hand reaching to position his beret. The light leapt in after him, a luminous rectangle that squatted on the floor. It stood out like an immobile chess square.

Light and dark, the two were alternating. The unreality of the situation was quickly giving way to a sense of fear. The wall behind us seemed to have grown to an opaque skyscraper, a damp vertical dividing continents, halving the world. The way out was tomorrow, a year, ten years too late. The other side of the building would give on to a new century, androids loading a silver truck with mannequins to be cerebralized with artificial intelligence.

'How did you kill him, you fags? You held him under and pushed him out to sea. Don't think we didn't see you do it. . . .'

Dione's words were left to resonate as unassimilable echoes. They hit the four walls and slapped our ears on the rebound.

The concentration had broken in one of his two companions. He had half turned round to follow the progress of the plane as it vibrated on the skyline. His blond, grizzled head showed black at the roots where the dye hadn't reached. His denim figure expressed not strength but an affected pose, the puffed-up body of a bird launching a territorial offensive. He had lapsed back into his natural posture; for that brief moment the aircraft had dispensed with his adopted masculinity. The gold cross he wore in his left ear glinted in answer to sunlight catching the streamlined aluminium tip of a wing.

Something was going to snap. The tension was at breaking-point. I could hear the whirr of a strap being flexed. Dione was still looking at us from another dimension, his eyes following his inner vision. I was looking out beyond him at a blue rift of sky as he tilted away to the left of my vision, Paul's leather belt slashing his cheek, his high-kicking follow-through scattering the two blonds, who offered no resistance.

We ran, the air hitting our lungs, the sea lifting to meet us as though we would fly into the incoming wave, our abrupt looping turn placing us back on the flat of the promenade in the direction of the gardens.

We eased up, as there was no one following us. Paul's adrenalin charge had abated. He took a deep breath as though finalizing the incident with his exhalation. It was an exorcism, a sharp, whistling rejection of the summer, of Dione's imposed tyranny.

We went up into our refuge and stood where the steps divided to right and left. On this stone platform facing the bay and under a slate and creeper-entwined shelter roof we had lived out the estranged journey of our youth. The sea was coming in. The clear, late-summer light framed everything in a gold translucency. I knew that Diana was down there on the promenade, searching, confused by my sudden flight. But that was for another time, another place. Rubella would find Dione and patch up his cosmetics, the welt incised on his cheek.

Paul took the path out of the gardens to the left, quick, resolved, not looking back. A radio was playing 'Walk on the Wild Side'. I went back in the direction of the town. We would all meet again, somewhere, somehow, perhaps years distant, coming out of the night, walking on a bridge over the star-pooled Seine, or bolting up from the Métro, late for an assignation, opportunely embracing a figure from the past across the bunch of scarlet carnations intended for another.

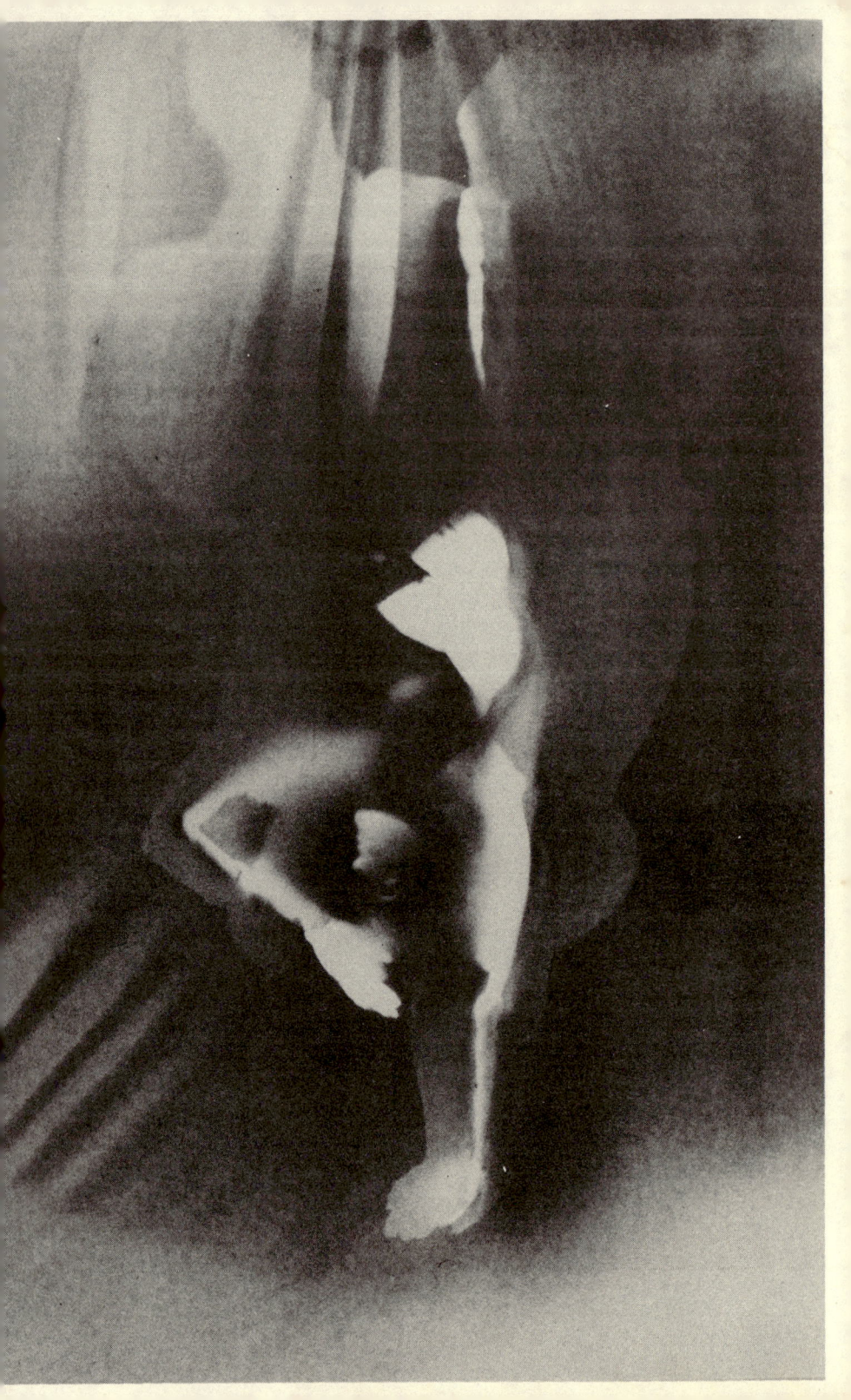